Cabana Boy

(Book Three of the Confessions of a Chick Magnet series)

by Jenny Gardiner

Chapter One

WHEN Fletcher Campbell first interviewed for the production assistant job with revered film producer Justine Gaynor, he was super excited at the prospect of attending poolside meetings as a perk of the job. After a succession of crap jobs waiting tables while trying to break into the film business, he figured this was payoff for his hard work and persistence.

"Everyone out here does them," she'd told him, arms spread wide at the outdoor café where she'd interviewed him. "No reason to waste this sunshine and warm weather!"

Which suited him just fine. After all, he loved spending time in nature. Having grown up in Montana, the outdoors was practically his middle name. He'd only moved out to LA after college to try his hand in the film industry, but he missed all that time he used to spend hiking and biking and kayaking and fishing. In LA, he devoted most of his time to sitting in traffic, sucking in exhaust fumes, which was painful for someone accustomed to the wide-open spaces around his hometown of Bristol, Montana. There, a hike in nearby Glacier National Park was as likely to yield a grizzly bear sighting as an outing in LA would involve a glimpse of a Kardashian or two. He'd take a bear over a Kardashian any day.

But this was the cost of pursuing a career in film. After being hired as an extra in a film shot on location in Glacier during freshman summer break, he'd become hooked on the business—even if he did end up on the cutting room floor. That was a memorable summer not only for his "star turn" as one of two hundred people in a crowd scene in the park but also because it was when he and Cricket Ferguson called it quits after having dated exclusively since the ninth grade. Ugh, he didn't want to think about the breakup. No matter how much time had passed, it still felt raw to him, with so many words left unspoken. But he was in LA now, with a new life, big dreams, and no need to waste time dwelling on what was. Or could have been.

At today's production meeting, scheduled at his boss's sprawling Beverly Hills mansion, he ended up being the only one in attendance besides Justine, who weirdly insisted on wearing a bikini even though she was well past the age—and youthful vigor—that justified voluntarily exposing so much flesh in a revealing bathing suit. It screamed "unprofessional," but who was he to know how things were out here? Oh well. If she was happy in it, that's what mattered.

Her pool—one of those elegant, sprawling, dark-bottomed Gunite types—boasted a waterfall and an actual bridge that bisected the whole pool. It was so large you needed a damned bridge to get to the other side; otherwise you'd be exhausted navigating your way around it. He'd never seen a backyard pool quite like this. Clearly he wasn't in Montana anymore. She'd dismissed her waitstaff of three as soon as they'd delivered drinks to the two of them, which was weird—day drinking during a business meeting? How very *Mad Men* of her! Good thing he could hang with the best of them after imbibing several drinks.

Fletch tried not to gawk at Justine as she perched, cross-legged on the overstuffed sofa beneath the shade of a massive umbrella, a floppy wide-brimmed hat cocked at an angle atop her head. Man, in the short time he'd been in LA, he'd never seen so many women overwrought in an attempt to defy aging, and Justine fit that bill perfectly. First off, bikinis weren't exactly forgiving when it came to hiding what nature hadn't gotten quite right or what time had done to a person. So while her surgically overhauled face was pulled so taut you could probably bounce a quarter off her cheeks, her neck was encircled with telltale sagging flesh that reminded him of the rings around a tree trunk that told you how old the thing was.

Granted, her arms were a testament to her personal trainer, who was usually leaving the office when Fletcher arrived each morning. Whatever that man was doing, he was making sure her guns were in tip-top shape. Same with her long legs, which he knew, along with her belly, had been CoolSculpted into cellulite-free existence. After all, he'd been the one stuck scheduling the expensive appointments. Her hair was the bleach white of those dying reefs you see in *National Geographic* specials about global warming. Her false eyelashes were so unnaturally long they could've derived from legs plucked from a daddy longleg, and she was spray-tanned to within an inch of her life.

Yet with all that work, maybe with the right clothing, you could possibly shave off ten years from your age, appearance-wise. But half-naked in a skimpy bikini? It all looked the opposite of young. Not that he was judging her. He was, however, getting the vibe that she had designs on him, and he wanted to be loud and clear that he had no plans to tangle up any sheets even if hers were the gold-karat-threaded, silk jacquard Charlotte Thomas ones, which cost more than his beat-up clunker of a truck. He should know—he was tasked with ordering her sheets, natch.

He'd had a fantasized notion of production assistants actually doing something involving producing, but in the few months since he'd been in the job, the only thing he'd done was his demanding boss's bidding. That meant chauffeuring her around LA because he was "far more handsome" than her regular driver. Fletch could only thank goodness for GPS given he'd hardly committed the geography to memory since arriving here, or they'd have been lost in the Hollywood Hills on more than one occasion. His other duty involved scheduling her weekly Brazilian wax, which bordered on TMI but he was trying to be a cooperative employee, so what was he to do?

Speaking of a Brazilian wax, her thong bikini bottom was cut high enough on her thigh and down toward her crotch that there was no question she'd made it to her appointment with Brigitte this week to ensure not a stray hair was to be had. Normally a teasing glance of that would have turned him on, big-time. After all, he'd helped Cricket do the honors—albeit with a razor—back when they were together. Shaving her there was the most erotic thing he'd ever done. But with Justine, ugh, he mentally shuddered. It would have been like lusting after someone's nana. In fact, she was pretty much old enough to be his grandmother. He squeezed his eyes shut at the thought.

"Fletcher, be a dear and help me get some sunscreen on," she said, waving the bottle of lotion at him. "Must fight these damaging UV rays." She winked at him and he winced, steeling himself to put sunscreen on her back and get out, soul intact. But in his gut, he knew that wasn't what she'd planned. He scraped his fingers through his wavy dark hair, knowing he had to suck it up and do it.

Standing, he walked to where Justine sat on the sofa and wondered where he was supposed to sit while doing this. It would be one thing if she were laying on her stomach. He'd squirt some lotion, politely dab it around, and beg off when it came to what to do with her thong-exposed butt cheeks. That was hers to figure out. But no. She was sitting there, her legs now extended, even spread a bit to his great dismay. Her ample fake tits—you could tell they were fake, not only because she was too old to have breasts perched so unnaturally high atop her chest, but also because of the telltale line that ridged her chest where a pouch of saline rested inside of each one—jutted out like the peaks of Everest and were equally as threatening to the uninitiated. And while her fabricated tits would look downright spectacular on someone half her age, on her, they smacked of desperation, a woman grasping at straws in the hopes that she could fool the general public that she wasn't as old as she was.

Yuck. It was all so icky. Why didn't women grow old gracefully out here? He thought about how pretty his own mother was, with her salt-and-pepper hair, which she wore in a bob cropped to her shoulder, and the laugh lines that life had given her lighting up her face with joy.

He didn't want to think about his mother's boobs, but he was certain they weren't parked on her chest like a diving board urging all comers to take the plunge. Geez, he'd take ten aging-gracefully women over one in-massive-denial-of-Father-Time version any old day. His mom was a grandma now and he saw how her grandchildren loved to press up against her soft body and snuggle into her loving warmth. Besides, every man knew that a little meat on the bones was an added bonus. Skin-and-bones ladies with zero percent body fat like Justine, whose hips jutted out like the jagged lines on a heart rate monitor, were a bit extreme; they didn't appeal to him.

He took a deep breath, pressing his blue eyes closed—the ones Cricket once said reminded her of precious sapphires. He almost wanted to plug his nose as if his mom was forcing the five-year-old version of him to down a forkful of stinky cauliflower. *Okay, Fletch. You can do this.* Unpleasant work have-to's were part and parcel to climbing the ladder in Hollywood. Not that he would succumb to a little slap and tickle with the woman to get his way—no way, no how—but capitulating when your boss coerces you into applying sunscreen didn't seem too far out of the ordinary.

"Uh, er, where did you want this?" He squirted some sunscreen into his hand, then leaned over her, figuring he'd go for the arms, which seemed a safe bet. How much trouble could he get into there? He stared at her wrist—far, far from even a hint of erogenous zones (although didn't Cricket love it when he stroked her wrist with his thumb?)—and began massaging in the lotion.

Justine let out a tiny moan.

Shit. Was this turning her on? He accelerated the application pace, moving his palms up her forearms, speed-slathering toward her bicep, hoping to the good Lord above that he could be done with this and get down to business. He'd have to lean over to reach the other arm, so he sucked it up and did it, gnawing on his cheek the whole time and averting his eyes. Anything to avoid coming in close contact with those prominent boobs, which seemed to be climbing toward him. When done with arm number two, he placed the bottle on the sofa next to her, hoping to return to his own seat, a safe several feet away.

But instead she pointed the toes on her right foot and extended her leg and foot toward his thigh, dragging her gelled toenails (he should know: he made the appointment) up his thigh till he thought he might scream.

6

Fletcher never thought the idea of a woman dragging a toe up his leg toward his dick would be a turnoff, but damn, when a granny substitute—and a bad one at that—was doing it, boy was it ever.

"You forgot these," Justine said, still flexing and pointing her foot as if that provocative move had any effect on him. Christ, what could he say? If he told her that was inappropriate, she'd fire him on the spot. If he proceeded on demand, his hands would end up sliding up her muscled thighs and practically smoothing over her pudenda. Ha! He hadn't thought of that term since the test on female anatomy in his middle school sex ed class. He could still picture an awkward Mrs. Rayburn with her pointer stick aiming at the illustration of the female anatomy on the board, and he cringed at the thought. He sure as hell couldn't mentally refer to this woman's thing as a "pussy." If he did, he'd never think of a pussy the same way again. Although he sure as hell wanted to think of a positive pussy to purge what he was doing from his mind. So he pretended he was slicking the sunscreen along Cricket's thighs, strong and sturdy from a lifetime of riding and living an outdoor life of hiking and running and mountain biking.

He closed his eyes. *Remind me again why I left Cricket for this?* He squirted some more lotion onto his hands and raced his fingers along his boss's legs and thighs, rapidly doing what he had to, just to get the chore over with. Now he understood that phrase, *lie back and think of England.*

Justine moaned again and suddenly ground her hips toward his hand, causing his fingertips to slip dangerously close to the thigh edge of her bikini. He feared he would throw up in his mouth. Real nanas didn't force guys young enough to be their grandsons to finger their twats. He pulled his hands away as if he'd touched a hot stove and dusted them off as though moving on to more important business.

"Okay. Well, then, weren't we here to brainstorm about the release of *Icicle Man*?"

This was Justine's latest film—something to do with a dude who froze to death in the mountains while searching for elusive clues to his own past. Right about now, Fletcher was putting his current fate up there with Icicle Man in the sucky outcomes department. Freezing to death almost sounded preferable to his current fate.

Just then Justine reached out her hand and pressed her palm to the crotch on the outside of his Chubbies trunks— the ones with the silverback gorillas all over them. If only he had the strength of a silverback; he'd knock her out of the way and run, far from this whacked-out woman. He tried to stick his butt out, away from her, to create distance so she couldn't grab his nuts next.

"Oh, have some fun," Justine said, dragging her shellacked sanguine nails along his thigh, making the hair stand on end. And not in a good way. His balls shriveled.

He had to think quickly, or this would only deteriorate into something even worse.

"It's only that my girlfriend—"

She lifted an eyebrow. "Girlfriend?" She waggled an admonishing finger. "And here I thought you were unencumbered." She thrust out her lower lip in a pout like she was a tween told she had an eleven-o'clock curfew.

He sucked so badly at lying, especially thinking on his feet like this. "Well, my girlfriend from back home, we decided to give it another go. And, well, I'm about to ask her to marry me."

Justine looked up, cocking her head like a cat toying with a mouse before killing it. "Marriage? How very provincial," she said. "Is that what they do wherever you're from?"

He squinted at her. "You mean get married?"

She nodded, once again dragging her daggers up his thigh, which made his abdomen contract from the chill it induced. "Aren't you too young for such adult things?"

Now that pissed him off. Too young to get married but not too young for a cougar thrice his age to come on to him like he was a slab of raw beef thrown at her? Yeah, right.

"I'm plenty old enough, thanks," he said, wiping the spare sunscreen off on his trunks as he delicately stepped back away from her.

"Where is this place you're from, where your girlfriend pines away for you?" She said it as though his life were some sort of amusement for her to play with like a toddler obsessed with the shiny bow on her Christmas present.

"I'm—we're—from Montana."

She turned her head up toward him. "Oh, really? One of those places with snowcapped mountains?"

He nodded and knit his brow, not knowing where she was headed with this. "Why do you ask?"

"Well, I think we've found where we're going to premiere our film!" She laughed. "We're going to Wherever-You're-From, Montana, and maybe then I can even have a word with that fiancée-girlfriend of yours."

Fletch's face fell. Shit. Fiancée-girlfriend. How was he going to get out of this—bringing his horny boss back home to size up what she saw as competition from a now-former lover (and never a fiancée) who could give half a shit about anything to do with Fletcher Campbell and would assuredly never cover for his lies. And to think he thought he'd been making progress professionally. *Sonofabitch.*

Chapter Two

CRICKET Ferguson finished mucking the stalls in the barn and decided to take a few minutes to enjoy the late-day sun as it cast its melon-hued light across the fields. Today was one of those days that reminded her why she wanted to spend the rest of her life in this amazing little hamlet she called home.

First she'd risen well before dawn, roused her Australian cattle dog, Dingo, for a four-mile run, a practice that cleared her mind and helped her plan her day. After returning home for a quick shower, she slipped down a flight of stairs to the pâtisserie she'd opened a year ago and got to work on the array of pastries and café food she'd planned to offer the good folks of Bristol today.

She and her close friend and assistant, Darby Cunningham had such fun working side by side it was a wonder that what she did was considered a job. After a couple of years of working for a succession of imperious pastry chefs, it took coming home and opening Pâtisserie Cricket to realize she was doing what she was always meant to do. Yeah, yeah, Pâtisserie Cricket was hardly the most French of names. But she needed to name her shop something as no-nonsense and basic as she was. Besides, this was Montana: not like anyone out here would be flocking to a shop with some hoity-toity French name. Here in Montana, folks wanted things to be simpler, and she was happy to offer that.

After spending the day creating and baking, she'd headed back to her parents' ranch and took a late-afternoon ride with her horse, a paint named Bunny, with Dingo running loops around them as they rode out past the hayfields and meadows and into the lush forest surrounding the farm. Riding in the woods during these autumn afternoons took her breath away, with the sumptuous palette of colors Mother Nature showed off, as leaves prepared to fall in anticipation of the first snowfall. This was God's country, so beautiful it almost hurt, and she loved every moment she could take in the splendor of it all. Despite her time in the cosmopolitan city of Paris while she trained, and then briefly along the East Coast afterward to get experience under her belt, this was the place that called to her. Sure, she'd needed to get away for a while after Fletch bailed on her. But now she'd wrestled with those demons, carved out a new life, and at last, everything was falling into place.

While she leaned against the split rail fence, her cowboy hat cocked on her head over her long, streaky blond hair, gnawing on a piece of straw and gazing out on the horizon, her phone dinged. She pulled it out to find a most unexpected email. It was from a big LA production company wanting to place an order for an obscene amount of food for a film premiere they were holding right here in little ole Bristol—a fantastic boon for her business. She'd talk to Darby first thing in the morning to plot out a strategy for handling the order before she replied to it in detail. While her business had been doing quite well, catering such event could put her on the map—not that she was looking to be put on a map. But still, anything like this could get word of mouth about her baking skills going beyond the borders of Bristol, and you never knew how that could benefit her fledgling pâtisserie.

After returning to Bristol last year, Cricket had been stuck for a while living at home, far past the point at which she'd hoped to be under her parents' roof. Finally this past summer, she and her dad had taken a sledgehammer to the room above the pastry shop and got to work creating a cozy apartment she could call her own. Each night when she went upstairs to her very own space, her heart sang. It was all she needed in life and she was, at last, content. This was no small feat after Fletcher Campbell crushed her hopes and dreams by blowing out of Bristol in pursuit of some pie-in-the-sky dreams of Hollywood fame and fortune. For the life of her, she didn't understand it, but she also couldn't stop it. Even though they'd talked for years about their future together—they'd even named their kids!—all of a sudden, poof, he was gone, leaving not a trace behind.

It had hurt at the time and was part of the reason she took off for Paris to learn to bake, but she also learned the hard way that with pain comes growth. There was little doubt she was almost over him and had practically grown ten feet tall in the process. And now she was perfectly content not to have any man getting in the way of her happiness. She had her shop, her apartment, and Dingo. Her life was full, and there wasn't room for another man in it even if she wanted one, which, after Fletcher, she decidedly didn't.

As Cricket read the email, she wondered for a moment if she was picking up some snark in between the lines.

"Cricket," it said. *"What a charming name. One of those names the boys probably love to bits."*

Whatever the hell that meant. What a weird comment for someone to make in a professional context.

"But I bet you don't even think about that, what with your fiancé and all. I'll look forward to sitting down with you and finding out

everything about you."

Cricket squinted. Fiancé? Huh? And why would she have any reason to find anything out about her? Maybe she was talking about her menu options? Or how she planned to serve it all at the film opening?

She shook her head. If there was one thing she'd learned since leaving Bristol for a while, it was that people were strange. Plenty were nice and normal and all that, but there were some weirdos out there, and she would chalk the comments up to that. After all, those rich Hollywood types were no doubt more likely to be a little more eccentric than your average Bristoller. Or was it Bristollian? She never did get that right.

Cricket thought about her name, which she always kind of liked, even though she never wanted to think about the genesis of it. The story was that she was conceived in a hayfield, with crickets trumpeting their horny mating call to the accompaniment of her folks doing the same damned thing—a fact that always made her roll her eyes. It's one thing if you're the one doing it in the hayfield, but your parents? Puh-lease. That's something you share on a need-to-know basis and she didn't need to know it. Nevertheless, she always thought the name Cricket had a nice ring to it.

Well, she'd dismiss the weird line of questioning about her name. And the fiancé reference. That woman—Cricket glanced down at her phone to see: Justine Gaynor—well, then, Justine Gaynor must have had that information flat-out wrong. She wondered why she surmised that, but figured it wasn't relevant. As long as she got this kick-ass order in and could fulfill it, the woman could call her the Queen of England.

She gave a whistle for Dingo and hopped into her truck, securing the dog into a doggy seatbelt before fastening her own. With a small laugh, she mused she had a huge event to plan for and wanted to get home to her mystery fiancé and get started on it.

Chapter Three

FLETCH never thought of himself as a buttoned-up, suit-and-tie type of guy, but after showing up at yet another poolside meeting as ordered in his swim trunks—this time the Cockatoodletoos (perhaps not the wisest ones to wear in Justine's presence, what with the suggestive title)—to find they were the only two meeting, he thought perhaps even a snowsuit might be in order. Better yet hazmat gear.

Yesterday Justine had tried to engage in a rousing round of find the salami, so Fletch was starting to have panic attacks every time he knew he would be alone with her, desperate to devise ways to stop her aggressive efforts to land him. Which was easier said than done with your boss's hand slipping beneath the thigh edge of your swim trunks as if it was a perfectly normal thing for an employer to do while discussing details of the press conference for the upcoming movie premiere. After all, who wouldn't grab for his dick under the circumstances? Said no one ever.

He looked forward to this premiere simply as a great excuse to get back home, take a bit of a breather from his libidinous boss, and ingest the fresh mountain air he hadn't realized he'd missed so much. He wondered if it would be possible to steer clear of Cricket while there. Part of him wanted to see her—it had been a long time, and he was curious how she was doing now. He'd heard from his mom that her pastry shop was the hit of the town. She always did love to bake back in the day. Oh well, no way would he step foot in there—she'd probably hit him with a rolling pin or something.

"I've had a few exchanges with your betrothed," Justine said as she absentmindedly scrolled through a text message on her phone. "Just finalizing the food for the event."

Fletcher turned his head quickly. "My betrothed? Finalizing food?"

Justine reached out a free hand and swirled the tip of her fingernail through the hair on Fletcher's inner thigh. The good news was there was no way he was going to get a hard-on under the circumstances. The bad news was his boss was fondling him, yet again. The worse news was she'd evidently gone behind his back to get hold of Cricket, and God only knew what that meant. He more than likely had already been busted in a huge lie he'd had to concoct to keep the woman at bay. So now what?

"What's her name again?" She lifted her hand in the air and snapped her fingers as if trying to recall. "Some sort of invertebrate, wasn't it?" She held up a finger. "Oh, yes, I remember. *Crick-et.*" She enunciated the syllables as if trying to remove a bad taste from her tongue.

Fletch blanched. "How did you—"

"A few strategically placed calls to the chamber of commerce and I was able to find your 'fiancée' with little effort." She made air quotes with the word "fiancée."

"About that—" Shit. This was the day he would be fired, right in time to skulk back home with no money and no job prospects. The good people of Bristol could laugh at his failed lofty ambitions. And he'd have to live in Bristol with Cricket, the successful businesswoman who hated the ground he walked on and would likely never speak to him even on his deathbed, which could be upon him, depending

16

on how furious Justine was about his dishonesty.

She stroked a finger over his lips and let out a shushing sound. "Nothing need be said. I can tell you two are keeping a tight lid on your betrothal. In fact, she barely responded when I mentioned her fiancé."

Fletcher had to think quickly on his feet. "It's complicated," he said. "There were things—"

"We can square away details later," she said, waving her hand in the air. "But for now, well, you're here, and I'm here, and you're a virile young man and I'm a woman in her sexual prime with certain needs—"

"About that." He took a few steps back, away from her octopus reach. "I think you'll understand that Cricket wouldn't be happy about this." He pointed back and forth between them. He wasn't sure what else to call it but for "this." Maybe sexual harassment? Assault with a deadly manicure? Better yet death by Horny Nana? He didn't doubt she was deadly—in a black widow kind of way. Didn't those venomous arachnids kill the male after mating? He shuddered—he could never consider sex with Justine mating. That would imply something copacetic about it.

Fletch decided to pull the oldest trick in the book and reached for his phone, pretending someone had been calling while his ringer was silenced.

"Hello?" He tucked his head down, then lifted his eyes toward Justine to see how closely she was watching. Luckily she'd taken this minute to reach for her champagne flute, an ever-present prop in her life. "Oh, hey babe. We were just talking about you." He glanced over to see that comment elicited a cocked eyebrow from the jezebel in the thong. "I'm so excited you'll be catering our event. Uh-huh. Uh-huh. Yep. Oh, crap. You need me to do that right now?" He nodded, engaged in a faux conversation that he prayed would help him get the hell out of here before he found himself pinned beneath the sharp hipbones of his predatory boss. He glanced at his watch. "Okay, well, I'm at work now, but I'm sure Justine will understand if I need to do that now. Love you, Boo Bear." He winked at Justine for good measure and made kissy noises into the phone, then made a point of pretending to hit the off button on the call.

"Sorry, Justine. Looks like I have to race over to the jewelers. The ring was being sized and Cricket wants me to bring it along when I head up there tomorrow." How the hell he was going to get Cricket to put on a ring from him was anybody's guess at this point. The whole thing was going to so blow up in his face and he hadn't a clue how to stop this train from careening into the station.

While he searched his brain for other excuses to get out of there, one of her staff approached and offered her a charcuterie plate.

"I'm famished, Paco," she said to him as she patted the empty seat next to her. "Why don't you join me and satisfy my hunger?"

Fletcher rolled his eyes and took advantage of the free moment to grab his keys from the table and make his way out of the lion's den. Looked like Paco was now at Justine's mercy, poor fellow.

"See you in a few days in Bristol?" he said as he picked up the pace and scurried away like a scared rabbit. Hell, he'd be in Bristol tomorrow. With a fake fiancée and a ring he needed to go find somewhere for cheap. What could possibly go wrong with such an ill-conceived plan?

Chapter Four

CRICKET was still trying to understand what it meant for Fletcher's boss to pretty much become her boss, what with this fat catering contract she couldn't turn down despite the weird conflict of interest. One thing she knew for sure: whatever that woman was saying about an engagement and that fiancé nonsense was gibberish. But if Fletcher was telling her tall tales to make himself look good or like a wholesome "family man"—no doubt something his boss valued in an employee—she wasn't going to contradict his words. At least not to her. Now if she got her hands on him in person, she'd likely go for full-on gullet throttle until she could find out what the hell had gotten into him. How dare he entangle her into his maddening web of deceit? Bad enough he left her to pursue his Cricketless Hollywood dreams, but then to make her part of his fake reality, well, that was so not cool.

Either which way, she was going to make a crapton of money on this gig and it was going to be pretty simple to execute. Plus, there was the cachet of catering a big Hollywood premiere—hard to put a price tag on that. Besides, Cricket was fairly certain she'd put enough emotional distance between Fletcher and her and she could do this without reopening painful wounds. No doubt it would be a real test of her mettle, but it would be good for her to know that she'd put her past behind her anyhow: an exercise in strength and restraint. Restraint from what—wanting to kiss him? Or hurt him the way he'd hurt her? She wasn't quite sure of the answer.

But then again… What if she had to deal with him? What if that Justine woman showed up and expected her and Fletcher to be all lovey-dovey? Could she do that to advance her business? Would she do that to help Fletcher further his career? The answer to number two was decidedly no. She had no interest in being some sort of savior to the guy. If it worked to her benefit, she'd play along. But as soon as it became something to save his sorry ass, she'd bail.

"Do you think I'm a complete schmuck for doing this?" Cricket looked over at Darby while piping crème pâtissière onto a layer of sponge cake for the Frasier cake she was constructing.

Darby, busy piping buttercream icing onto raspberry and cream cupcakes, thrust out her chin. "Well, it depends on your definition of schmuck." She paused to fill the icing bag as she glanced over at her friend with a broad smile.

"Ha ha. Very funny. I mean it. Maybe I should tell this Justine woman thanks but no thanks and get on with things. Keep it all clean and Fletcher-free for my own sanity."

She piped carefully between each of the strawberries that were propped side by side and upright on the inside edge of the springform pan, being sure to fill all the gaps. When this cake was finished, it would be a beautiful showpiece birthday cake for one of her favorite customers. She placed more sliced berries atop the swirl of pastry crème, then piped one more layer of crème, smoothing it evenly before settling the second half of the sponge cake atop it. Gently she pressed on it to nestle the entire creation within the walls of the cake pan, then topped it with a thin disk of marzipan. She carried the cake to the walk-in fridge to allow it to set, grabbed the pastry dough that had been chilling, and started to roll it out for lemon curd tarts, her special of the day.

"If you want to know what I think, and I know you do because I'm your best friend and my opinion rates"—she winked—"I say you take Fletcher out of the equation altogether. He's over and done with. Why let his existence even matter? So you get this once-in-a-lifetime client who will pay you lots of money. You'll let your skills shine, make lots of money, and maybe land some other big clients afterward. Ultimately I think you'll be 'Fletcher who?' It's been a long time, Crick. You outgrew him anyhow and you don't need him. To be honest, it sounds like he needs you and that's a fun position to be in. You can thumb your nose at him—or flip your finger, whichever you'd rather—and he simply doesn't matter!"

Cricket reached for a spoon, scooping it into the waiting bowl of lemon curd then popping it into her mouth. "I guess it's a bit like this curd: the lemon on its own is sour and almost inedible," she said, licking her lips as she savored one of her favorite tastes. "But combined with the right ingredients, it's a winning proposition. Amiright?"

Darby grabbed another spoon and dipped it in for a sample. "That's the spirit, Cricket. You can get through this and be a better woman for it."

Cricket wanted badly to believe her friend was right. But it had been a long damned time since she'd been in Fletcher's presence, and she worried she'd feel that old magnetic pull that had made them such a dynamic couple in the first place. Like it or not, she was about to find out. The chances of her avoiding him were pretty much nil.

Chapter Five

FLETCHER peered out the window at the nearby mountain peaks as his plane approached Kalispell City Airport. He'd still have an hour drive to get to Bristol from here, but the minute he saw the pristine lakes and jagged peaks of the Rocky Mountains at 30,000 feet, a familiar warmth settled in that he realized had been missing from his life. He'd spent much of his upbringing wandering through Glacier National Park, hiking rugged trails to crystal blue icy lakes, following narrow footpaths in search of elusive bighorn sheep. This place could not have been more different than Los Angeles—so much so that he'd started to wonder what exactly drove him to the crowds and traffic of that sprawling metropolis when he felt a natural pull to this breathtaking wilderness right in his own backyard.

The nice thing about small airports like Kalispell is you could touch down, get your bags and your rental car, and be on your way within half an hour. Before he knew it, he was already on the two-lane country road that would take him home to Bristol. Despite the early autumn chill, he powered his windows down and took in the fresh mountain air, and a smile spread across his face. This was almost perfect: not a perverted boss to be found and no wasted time scheduling Justine's next vanity appointment to remove cellulite or inject poison into her face to fight wrinkles. Instead it was just him and his happy place, all to himself. This was going to be a great trip.

Not fifteen miles before reaching town, he had to stop his car to wait for a moose to cross the road. He laughed out loud, imagining such a thing occurring on the freeway in LA. It was good to have this little moment of cheer before he arrived in town. His first order of business would be breaking it gently to the girl he left for his supposed glamorous Hollywood career that he needed her to pretend they were engaged to save him from being sexually harassed by his boss. His gut told him this was not going to go over well with her.

Once he entered the commercial district of Bristol, he pulled his rented SUV into the first space he could find and got out, stretching his legs after all of the traveling. It would be a couple of blocks' walk to Cricket's shop—not that he'd been there, but his mother had told him where it was located. This way he could stroll down Main Street and muster his courage a bit before steeling himself for the confrontation. Not that it had to be a skirmish, though it likely would be.

As Fletch wandered down Main Street, he waved at familiar faces, poking his head into Jackson's Barber Shop and at the Great Outdoors Wilderness Shop where he'd spent more money than he cared to imagine over the years. He passed by Dr. Eliasson's veterinary clinic, then by Harry's, a rooftop bar he was known to frequent plenty. So much familiar territory here, yet he was removed from it right now. Everyone here had moved on without him, which made him a bit sad. Or had he moved on without them?

He passed by Annie Bananie's Pie Emporium and made a mental note to swing back later for a slice of Annie's triple-berry pie with lattice crust. It was the kind of dessert that made you lick the plate, and what self-respecting person could resist that? Maybe he'd bring a whole pie home for his mom for dessert. She'd like that.

He took a deep breath. Autumn had settled in here in Bristol—snow would be here soon. The smell in the air told him as much. He loved Bristol blanketed in snow and the locals all jazzed to get back up on the mountain to tackle the slopes. It was always the best between-tourists season—the summer

thrill seekers and camper van tourists long gone, the skiers and snowboarders not yet invading the place. That's why all the diehards lived here even when it became deathly cold or when the locals were snowed in. He struggled to find a similar charm about Los Angeles. Sure, the beaches and the Pacific Ocean were amazing. And a sunny, eighty-degree day in LA with low humidity was hard to beat, but it couldn't hold a candle to a day on the mountains here even if it was sleeting. Returning to Bristol reminded him that this place was in his bones.

Fletcher turned right off of Main Street onto Mulberry and looked up to see his old girlfriend's pride and joy. He could hardly believe it—Pâtisserie Cricket painted above the storefront same as you'd see at a traditional Parisian boulangerie and pâtisserie, telling all the world that his girl had moved on, far away from him. From plain old Cricket to a gifted chef who had the balls and temerity to open up her own shop when others in their peer group were still putzing around with lackluster careers that seemed to be going nowhere fast. His included. He was Justine's glorified manservant, no closer to a career in the film business than if he were working at a movie theater. The realization punched him hard, right in the solar plexus: Cricket had moved on to bigger and better things without him, and he was trapped as a lackey. Somewhere in the back of his mind, he was starting to doubt his decision to end things with her after all.

His heart raced a bit as he followed the brick walkway to the entrance. On one side near the large bay windows, stood a display of bread with Halloween images stenciled in flour on top of each loaf: a cat with its back arched, a jack-o'-lantern, a ghost. But beyond the bread were rows of brightly colored pastries that made his mouth water in an instant. He was tempted to turn around and leave, ashamed at how far Cricket had come and how low he'd sunk. But he had no choice; like it or not, he needed her help to save his ass.

A bell jangled loudly as he opened the beveled glass and wood door, which didn't help matters. The last thing he wanted was for attention to be instantly focused on him before he had a chance to get the lay of the land. He entered to see three wide cases filled with vibrantly colored pastries, tarts, and cakes, with the wall behind the counter stocked with bread in varying shapes and sizes. Incredible.

"Can I help you?"

Fletch looked up to see a familiar-looking woman with long red hair and bright blue eyes squinting at him.

"Darby?" He furrowed his brow. "What the hell are you doing here?"

She crossed her arms and arched a brow at him. "Fletcher Campbell? I'd say that question is reserved for you."

Fletch scrubbed his hand over his face. Little did he know Cricket would have reinforcements in the form of Darby Cunningham, her best friend from childhood. He hoped pastry shops, unlike butcher shops, were short on knives as he was fairly certain Darcy had figuratively thrown a slew of daggers his way in the process of helping her friend heal over the breakup.

Pursing his lips, he tried to figure out what to say. He

needed to save his hard-core apologies for Cricket. As he toed the ground along the base of one of the pastry cases, he spoke quietly. "Any chance Crick's around?"

She glared at him. "So you can say or do something super shitty that I'll be stuck having to mend? Thanks but no thanks, Fletch."

He shook his head. "Look, I know you don't think too highly of me—"

She scoffed at him.

He held his palm up and moved it back and forth as if erasing his words. "Okay, I know you think I'm a flaming asshole."

She nodded. "That's a start."

"And you're certainly entitled to that belief." He avoided eye contact with her and instead stared at the pastries that looked pretty fucking amazing. A fantasy of Cricket toiling away over each perfect little gem of a dessert ran through his head. He had no idea she was so gifted.

"Ding ding ding," she said. "Now what is it you want?"

"I need to talk to Cricket."

"Are you planning to mess with her head? Because if you are, I am so not going to let you know where she is. And I will personally see to it that you don't step foot in this shop ever again."

He rolled his eyes. Was this the police interrogation before the real police interrogation from Cricket herself? He held up his hands. "It's all good. I'm not here to undermine Cricket or cause problems, but I need to talk with her. Please." Cocking his head, he widened his eyes.

"Is there a problem?"

Fletcher lifted his head to see Cricket standing across from him, not two feet away, even more beautiful than he remembered her if that was possible. She wore a white apron, but it didn't obscure that gorgeous figure he remembered well—those round, firm breasts, that narrow waist, and that scrumptious ass he once so loved to squeeze. She wasn't the girl he'd remembered but had grown into a woman he'd not soon forget. Her long hair was pulled into a side braid that draped over her shoulder. Her sea green eyes were still stunning, even if they did glower at him.

"Uh, yeah, there's a big problem," Darby said, pointing at him with excessive dramatic flair. "Begins with an F, followed by L, E, T, C, H, E, and R."

Fletch frowned. "Your guard dog has been doing a fine job of protecting you."

Cricket lifted a brow. "Great. Then I chose wisely. Unlike the last time I trusted someone to care for me. We all know how that panned out."

Fletch raised his hands as if he was about to be arrested. "Okay, okay. I deserve all of your barbs. From both of you. I admit it. I'm an asshole. I've done hurtful things. I suck. I don't deserve empathy or kindness from either of you." He looked from one to the other and placed his hands on the glass case separating him from the two women. "But I'm going to tell you why I'd be super hugely extremely massively grateful if you might consider extending me the courtesy, even if it goes against every grain in your body. I need your help. Badly."

Chapter Six

CRICKET stared into Fletch's blue eyes and a pang of sadness washed over her. Those were the eyes she'd stared into so lovingly for so long, yet they were gone in the blink of, well, an eye. And here they were as though no time had elapsed. As if nothing had changed. Even though of course it had. So very much. And here he was, almost groveling. She couldn't imagine what would compel him to show up after all this time and beg like this.

The bell rang and Mrs. Rendleman, the school's band director, walked in.

"Hi ladies!" she said, turning to see who they were talking to. "Why, Fletcher Campbell? What are you, of all people, doing here?" Her eyes opened wide as she stared at Cricket trying to convey some sister power thing to her or something.

"Oh, hey Mrs. R," Fletch said. "Great to see you. Hope your eighth-period study hall is going well these days."

Which almost made Cricket laugh. The two of them used to slip out of study hall during eighth period and make out in the janitor's closet on the third floor. She threw him the side-eye instead.

"Darby, would you mind helping Mrs. Rendleman while I see what Mr. Campbell wants?"

She knew that was a caustic swipe referring to him that way, but oh well, it was the least she could do. She crooked her finger at him, indicating he should follow her back to her office. They walked through a set of double doors into the kitchen, then off to the right back corner, where she had a small office that consisted of a desk piled with papers and a folding chair next to the desk, also piled high with papers. Dingo, who'd been curled up in a ball on her bed, stood up and snarled at Fletch. What a good girl she was, warning her enemies to steer clear!

"Um—" He nodded to her.

"Looks like Dingo can distinguish friend from foe." She reached into a bag on her desk and pulled out a dog cookie. "Good girl." The dog came right up to her and wagged her tail as Cricket fed her the treat.

"You got a dog," he said.

"Astute observation." She curled up the side of her mouth in a "no duh" gesture.

"Okay to pet her?"

"At your own risk." Cricket was rather enjoying making him uncomfortable. The dog growled quietly. "Dingo, no. I know your gut is telling you otherwise, but this man is okay. For now, at least." She motioned to Fletch. "Go ahead, pet her."

"With that ringing endorsement—"

"Oh don't be a pussy," she said. "When has a growling dog ever made you scared?"

"When said dog belongs to a woman I jilted a long time ago."

She nodded. "Jilted, indeed. But I don't as a rule encourage my dog to maim people. Hold out your hand, keep your fingers tucked in, and let her sniff you."

He did as he was told and after about ten seconds, Dingo stopped growling and let him scratch her head. But like her owner, she didn't seem particularly receptive about it—not a tail wag to be seen. *Good girl.*

Cricket nodded for Fletcher to sit on the folding chair, so he bent down and lifted the stack before plopping down onto it, then rested her pile of paperwork on his lap. All things considered, it was good to make him a little uncomfortable.

She took off her apron, hanging it on a hook behind her desk, opened her laptop, and checked a few messages while he began to talk. She wanted to send the message that he was not a priority in her life.

"So. To what do I owe this, dare I say 'pleasure'?" She snarled a lip at the notion as she air quoted the word.

Fletcher's jaw muscle flexed and he was no doubt clenching his teeth. He had a little scruff on his face that looked impossibly sexy. Cricket hated herself for thinking that too. She also hated herself for thinking about the razor burn that would cause if say, he reached over and pulled her in for a kiss—one of those kisses like they did back then, where you can't help but merge your mouths and your breathing becomes one and you aren't quite sure where one of you begins and the other one ends.

Taking a deep breath, Fletch paused. "I understand you've been communicating with my boss," he said with a frown.

Cricket gave a tight smile. "Would that be a woman named Justine?"

He nodded slowly. "One and the same."

"The very Justine who referred to me as your fiancée?"

He rolled his eyes this time, and that ticked her off. Like that was such a far-fetched notion he had to punctuate it with that gesture? Jerk.

"I'm truly sorry about that. It's a funny story—"

Cricket steepled her hands and rested her chin on her

fingertips. "Oh, goodie. I love a funny story. Do tell."

She couldn't help the sarcasm bleeding from her like a sucking chest wound. It was time for him to pay—for something, somehow.

"Justine is, well, she's... actually she's, uh, creepy."

Cricket furrowed her brow. This wasn't what she expected to hear. "Huh?"

"I spend the better part of my workday fending off sexual advances from her," he said. "To be perfectly honest, I had to concoct a lie to keep her away from my johnson."

"Look, Fletcher, if you are having sex with your boss, I would appreciate you taking this elsewhere and not embroiling me in your weird stuff, 'kay? It was hard enough getting over you, but to think about you sleeping with women in LA, particularly your boss, well, it's so not cool to come here and drive the nail in deeper."

He shook his head vigorously. "This isn't to make you upset or angry or anything," he said. "I need you to know I didn't make things up out of nothing. I mean seriously, this woman makes me wear bathing suits to meetings and schedules them when we'll be all alone at her private swimming pool, and then she dismisses the waitstaff and it's just me and she'll make me put sunscreen on her and then when I'm up close she slides her fingers up my swim trunk leg and—"

Cricket made a mimicking gesture with her hands. "And then she stroked her hand along my hard length and spread my seed across the head of my cock and that's when I told her I had to have her right then and there." She continued. "Blah blah blah, I couldn't control myself, I mean what man could turn down a woman who is seducing you like that, blah blah blah, so I fucked her because that's the type of guy I am."

Fletch paused and stared at her. "Do you honestly think I'm that much of a prick?"

Cricket paused. She wasn't sure what she thought. She'd spent such a long time vilifying him in a vague way, who Fletcher actually was had gotten lost in the midst of it all. He'd become lore, only not in a good way.

"Well? Do you? If you do, then you sure as hell don't know me, and clearly you never did. Though I made decisions that hurt you, I did what I thought was best for both of us at the time, and I didn't do it to be a huge dick to you. I was trying to make a clean break so that neither of us had regrets. But simply because I might have handled that in a less-than-stellar manner doesn't mean I'm a bad person. Right now I am dealing with a boss who doesn't understand what the word 'no' means and I'm trying desperately to keep what little dignity I have remaining, but it's even harder to do that when you think I'm here with some agenda or ulterior motive."

Cricket heaved a sigh and rested her chin on her hand. "All right. Fine. So, to get this straight: you're telling me that basically your boss is sexually assaulting you on a regular basis and the only way you could think of to get her off your back was to lie and tell her you had a fiancée, who unfortunately became me."

He nodded slowly. "That sounds stupid, doesn't it?"

"Gee, ya think?" She pursed her lips. "And exactly how did it go from this little fake storyline to Justine arranging for me to cater a film premiere?"

He shrugged. "She's manipulative, that's how. She started doing her due diligence and found out about you—about us—and I'm guessing this was a way for her to dig her claws in and find out more about my life and how to maybe double-cross you for being engaged to me—I know, even

32

though that was a complete lie—and, well, she's an even better liar. Maybe she knows when others are lying?"

"So what does this mean for me, right here and now?"

He glanced up at her, looking like a sheepish kid who got caught having broken the window with his baseball, then rifled around in his pocket, pulling out a ring.

"I don't suppose you'd agree to wear this for a couple of days while Justine is in town? Maybe save me from her roving hands and allow me to keep my dignity?"

Cricket glared at him. "You have got to be kidding me." She stared at the stupid ring. "I mean, really, Fletcher?" She never ever called him by his full name—he was always Fletch to her. And she knew he would read the negative vibes in her wording. "Do you have any idea how long it took me to get over you? And now you want me to pretend we're something we're not? What about everyone in town? They'll all be asking me about this idiotic ring and it's bad enough I have to share the air with you in Bristol while you're here, but now I have to share a life with you?"

Fletcher winced. "I can't even begin to describe what it feels like to have your boss's fingernails stroking along your cock. How violating it is. Look, I'm trying to get ahead professionally, keeping my head down, and working hard. But I'm being thwarted by this horny woman old enough to be my grandmother trying to get with me."

Cricket shook her head. "Dude, get in line. You're describing something that probably ninety percent of women have experienced at least once. This is nothing new. It's just less common for a man to deal with it. I had a boss in Paris who daily came up behind me and pressed his erection into my ass. But I didn't make anyone pretend we were getting married because of it."

"Look, Crick. I know the last person in the world you

want to do anything nice for is me. And while I'm sad about that, I completely understand. But if you can find it in your heart to do this, I will be forever indebted to you."

She stood up, leaning over, her hands resting on a pile of papers on her desk. She liked this power position over a groveling ex who'd left her in a position of pain and weakness for so long. In all truth though, it wasn't her jam to be a jerk to the guy. Well, maybe at one point she would have. But not now. She'd once loved him with all her heart, and for that, he'd always own a little piece of it. And she couldn't turn away someone who'd played such an important role in her life. Even if it was going to be super awkward and she was going to likely regret this after he returned home and left her having to explain away yet again how they actually were no longer a couple, even though this time it would only be a fake one.

She heaved a sigh. "Doing this goes against every instinct in my body, Fletcher. And let me make it clear to you: the only reason I'm agreeing is because you were an important piece of my life for a long time. I can't undo that, nor can I take away that for a long time you were the love of my life. Yes, you hurt me terribly, but I'm over it and even stronger for it. And I certainly don't benefit by denying you something that matters to you."

Fletch clasped his hands together. "Thank you, Cricket. Thank you so much." He stood to hug her and she pushed him away.

"But," she said, hesitating. "There will be ground rules. One is that there will be no physical contact—"

"That's impossible if we're to be believable as a couple who's getting married."

She shrugged. "That's yours to figure out. I'll fake it but I won't—I can't—be all lovey-dovey with you. It would resurrect too much and I don't want to revisit some of the most painful parts of my life, thanks. Ultimately this means we appear together as little as possible—and I can blame my work for that, which is entirely believable. If this is a no-go for you, well, then, so be it. If you wanted someone who was going to be all over you, you should've found yourself an escort service for hire."

He thrust his lower lip out in a pout. "I guess I'll take what I can get," he said, disappointment written on his fallen face. "But you'll put the ring on at least?"

She rolled her eyes. Ugh. Some cheap, cheesy engagement ring from Fletcher? Really? "All right. Fine. But it better not give me a rash—I know you probably got this stupid thing out of a gumball machine and it's going to be bad enough wearing it, let alone if it causes me skin problems. I'll wear it when we're together and if your boss is nearby. And if I take it off, it's because I'm cooking and I never wear my rings when I'm in the kitchen. Deal?"

He nodded slowly, then reached out his hand to shake hers. "I know you said no touching, but can we at least shake on it to make it official?"

She extended her arm slowly as he reached to slide the ring onto her left ring finger. Her breath hitched in her throat—there was a time this moment would have been the pinnacle of her dreams, a forever future with the man she loved with such intensity it was almost overwhelming. And while she wanted to say that at this very moment, she felt at best ambivalence and at worst disgust, she'd be lying. Instead, her heart was pounding a staccato beat all the way up in her throat, and she could feel a flush of red scurry up from her chest, past her neck, and across her face. For the first time, she sensed the warmth of his hands on hers and could only remember how his touch had aroused her, gave her goose bumps, made her think only the dirtiest of thoughts about what she would do to him once she got her hands on him in private. Too bad those thoughts were so not part of the new deal between them. She looked down at her flour-stained shirt to see her nipples standing at attention through the flimsy jersey fabric that was right now betraying her thoughts to her former lover. And she wondered if her body might be on to something. It had been an awfully long time since she'd been with a man, and maybe this fake engagement thing would be a prime time to conduct a fake affair with her fake fiancé. After all, why not kill all birds with one stone? She shook her head against the thought.

"Oh, and one more thing," he said.

She squinted at him, worried about whatever bomb he was going to drop on her now. "Ugh. What now?"

"Just so you know, my pet name for you is Boo Bear."

Well, geez. This was going to be the longest week of her life.

Chapter Seven

THE one other takeaway from Mrs. Rayburn's sex ed class in middle school was that the human body had all sorts of ways of broadcasting things someone's head might not ever want anyone to know. One only need look at every boy in junior high school to know this: walking around with a textbook strategically placed over his crotch in an attempt to disguise the burgeoning hard-on that he couldn't help and desperately wanted to rein in but couldn't.

So looking at Cricket's involuntary response to his merely placing his hands on hers was telling: her nipples were standing at attention, and it wasn't because she was cold. At least he hoped it wasn't. She was turned on... as turned on as he was at the feel of her skin on his. His heartbeat raced a bit and, astonished, he blinked a few times. When he broke things off with her, it wasn't because he was no longer attracted to her, but rather because he was trying to do what was right—not lead her on and think they could conduct their relationship long-distance. He made a clean break of things to spare her the sadness and yearning that would no doubt overwhelm her. It always did for the one who got left behind. And he couldn't drag her along with him to LA. After all, he was going to be caught up focusing on his career, and it would be too expensive for her to come along. Besides, Cricket belonged in Montana. It was where her heart was. Until it wasn't—hadn't she hauled off to Paris in no time flat after he'd pulled out of Bristol?

He was trying to make sense of her response when he heard someone call his name as he was walking back to his car. He turned to see Darby hot on his heels, waving her hand at him.

"Darby?" He stopped to let her catch up.

She came to an abrupt halt in front of him, sweeping her hair out of her eyes as she caught her breath.

"Look, Fletcher." She pointed back in the direction of the pâtisserie. "I'm not quite sure what went on back there, but I want to warn you off of Cricket. It took her a long time to finally get over you, and I will personally slice both of your gonads off and shish kebab them in front of everyone at the park in the center of town over an open firepit if you do anything to hurt her, break her heart, lead her on, or make her think that she somehow matters to you. Do I make myself abundantly clear?"

His eyes grew wide. "Well, shit, Darby. How do you really feel about me?"

"Frankly, Fletcher, I don't feel particularly warm and fuzzy toward you. What you did—or at least how you did it—was completely shitty and as one who helped Cricket pick up the pieces after you left, I don't ever want to see her go through something like that again. You had your shot at her, but she's no longer yours and I don't want you entertaining the notion that she might be, even for a couple of days. Got it?"

Fletcher tilted his head to the side. "You got me, Darbs. My plan was to come back and use and abuse Cricket since she's low-hanging fruit. Because, well, you know that's so like me."

She shook her head. "I don't know what you're like. I know we thought you played fair and square until you didn't.

So now I want to be clear that Cricket's heart is not something to trifle with. As long as you honor that request, then you and me"—she pointed at him, then at herself—"will be fine."

Fletcher reached out and put his hands on Darby's shoulders. "You know what? Sometimes a young man has to figure his shit out. And sometimes when that man does that, he doesn't even know what shit he has to figure out. And sometimes he thinks he's being honorable when it turns out he's being an asshole. And sometimes that man matures and never actually realizes the extent to which he was an asshole." He wiped his brow with his wrist. "So yeah, maybe I mishandled things. Maybe I was unnecessarily hurtful to Cricket. But in all honesty, do you think I aimed to be as big a dick as possible to her? I mean come on, Darby. You knew me your whole life. Was I the one who drove you to the hospital every day for three weeks when your sister had that riding accident and was all plastered up like a zombie with her leg sticking up in the air and stuff?" He extended his arms and a leg as if he was in traction. "Do you honestly think I'm some evildoer back to exact revenge for Lord knows what?"

Darby placed her hands on her hips, scrunched up her nose, then shook her head. "Hell, Fletch. I don't know what your deal is. I only know what I dealt with after you broke up with my best friend. And I don't want that to happen again. So if your intentions are honorable, then fine. But Just. Don't. Hurt. Her. And we'll be good. Fair enough?"

He shook his head. Damn, who knew he was going to be grilled by the damned FBI about something he did when he was still practically a kid?

"Deal." He reached out and the two shook hands. "Now go tell Boo Bear to remember her engagement ring at the reception tomorrow night."

She cocked her eyebrow. "Boo Bear?"

He shook his head as he rolled his eyes. "Seriously. Don't ask."

Fletcher spent the next day preparing for Justine's early afternoon arrival. He made sure the overpriced inn where she was booked had precisely four overflowing arrangements of fresh flowers in her room. He then ensured that she had an unlimited supply of alkaline water and that room service would provide a broad selection of paleo options because, well, Justine. You didn't keep a body like that as thin as a mink pelt without a permanent diet plan.

He checked the setup for the ballroom at the old-fashioned movie palace where the film would be shown. He wanted to be certain the speakers were working fine with the mics. Justine was so exacting that if anything backfired there would be hell to pay and he'd be the one paying it.

He had a driver picking her up at the airport and knew she'd insist on a meditation hour upon arriving at the inn. He pretty much begged the innkeeper to make sure their dog didn't bark and that no one rang the doorbell during that time. Following that, he'd lined up a personal Pilates instructor for her for an hour, so that took care of much of the time leading up to the reception, one of two that Cricket would be catering. His goal was to keep Cricket and Justine as far away from each other as possible. He had to get through tonight's event, then the premiere on Friday and all would be good. All while trying hard not to think about Cricket's hard nipples, which kept his dick on high alert each time he remembered it.

Jesus this was going to be a hard damned week to navigate without a massive implosion.

Chapter Eight

CRICKET and Darby were putting the finishing touches on the food before transferring it to the Orion Theater, which was conveniently a few doors down from the shop.

"So I noticed you chased after Fletch yesterday after he left," Cricket said as she shifted mini quiches to one of the boxes in which they'd haul everything over there. "Did I miss anything interesting?"

Darby licked a dab of icing off her hand as she finished icing some mini cupcakes. "I wanted to let him know that I was watching out for your welfare, that's all."

"Darb, you know I'm fine, right? You don't have to worry about me anymore. I know I went through a tumultuous time of it, but look at me." She spread her arms out. "I've got this amazing shop and I get to work at it with my best friend. Customers love the place. I have the best dog on the planet"—she gave a whistle to get Dingo to come—"and now I'm catering my ex-boyfriend's perverted boss's film premiere week, knowing full well that she will stop at nothing to get that man in bed with her. All while I have decided that I think I want to end up in bed with him."

Darby's eyes grew wide. "Please tell me you're fucking joking."

Cricket stopped what she was doing and looked at her friend. "D—I was thinking about this. I mean, it's been a ridiculously long time since I've been with a man. That can't be good for me, can it? Isn't there some use-it-or-lose-it rule with erogenous zones?"

Darby laughed as she dusted some confectioner's sugar off Cricket's cheek. "You mean if you don't have a partner-prompted orgasm every so many months, you'll never have them again?"

"Make that every so many years."

"Oh, come off it, Crick. You've been with other guys since Fletcher Campbell."

She shrugged. "Well, yeah, early on there were a small number of revenge fucks along the way," she said. "Shame was he never knew about them, so a lot of good that was. In any case, once the charm of taking revenge wore off, I never happened upon someone with whom I had that sort of sexual chemistry since Fletch."

"But you wouldn't seriously consider a fling with him now, right?" She knit her brows.

Cricket grinned. "Sometimes a girl's gotta scratch an itch, you know? And what better itch to scratch? First off, I'm over him. So it would be purely sexual in nature. And it would be easy since there would be no fumbling and figuring each other out. We *know* each other that way. I'm sure it would be like getting back on a bike."

"Yeah well, there would be the riding aspect."

"Like I said, sounds perfect. Don't you agree?"

Darby shook her head vigorously. "No! It sounds like the stupidest idea I've heard in a long time. It's bad enough you two are pretending to be getting married. Like, *what the actual fuck* stupid? I still don't get that whole thing and how that is going to happen. Far be it from me to worry about that. It's your gig. But to complicate matters by having actual sex?"

"Maybe you should reframe this to see it better. We'll

pretend we're having sex, so we might as well have sex. See what I mean?"

"Why are you so intent on getting laid all of a sudden?" Darby stacked a box of mini cupcakes on one of the café tables near the door. "We have so many hot-looking guys coming through this town all the time. They're here to hike and bike and kayak and ski and snowboard. Why none of them?"

Cricket heaved a sigh. "Because he touched my hand."

Darby's brows ski-sloped into one another. "Come again?"

"Yesterday, when we were talking. And he pulled out that stupid ring, and he touched my hand as he put it on and it evoked so many things I'd forgotten about—emotions I'd blocked out, sure, but also memories of amazing times with him. And not regular old times, but I remembered that we fit so well together sexually. As I said, I'm over him. But the idea of that part of him, with me, that sounds like what the doctor ordered."

"I didn't know the doctor had diagnosed you with some problem that only Fletcher could solve."

"Right now, what Fletcher could solve is this horniness that seems to have come out of freaking nowhere and thanks to that, I can barely rub my legs together without getting off."

Her friend plugged her ears and started chanting *la-la-la-la-la*. "Need-to-know basis."

"Well, you asked."

"Nevertheless." She jutted her chin out. "I want to protect you from him and from yourself. You *think* you're over him, but if I were a betting woman, I'd put money on you not being quite as over him as you think you are. I mean, let's be real. Fletcher is a handsome man. He's got a great

44

body and a charming demeanor. He's smart, funny, and kind. Well, except when he fucked you over the way he did. But pretty much on a pie chart, for the most part, he'd be like a big old chunk of bright blue."

"Pie chart? Bright blue?" Cricket squinted at her trying to interpret that. "Whatever. At any rate, these are all arguments for me being safe for the time being. I'll get it out of my system and all will be fine."

Darby held up her hands. "Okay. I give up. You're going to do what you're going to do. But please, don't come crying to me when this blows up in your face."

Cricket started to load boxes onto the wheeled cart they would use to move the food over to the theater. "I promise. I'm a big girl now. It'll be fine."

The party was in full swing—everyone of note from Bristol had been invited to attend. Cricket could barely walk five feet without someone talking to her. She tried to keep her left hand down by her side to avoid questions from anyone who might see her faux engagement ring. She also tried to steer clear of Fletcher, who seemed glued to the side of Justine, appropriately dressed in a form-fitting animal print with spots on it. Cougar, thy name was clearly Justine. It was quite obvious that Justine was trying to stake her claim on Fletch, with her hands pawing at him—pressed to his chest, her palm at the base of his back, stroking down his arm, drawing her daggered claws along his jawline. She was a charmer, that one was.

Cricket went back to the staging area to check on the waitstaff to be sure everything was under control.

"Go," Darby said, swishing her away. "We've got this under control back here. Go mingle with people and enjoy your moment to shine."

"You sure?"

"Yes, of course. It's all fine. Go find your fiancé. I'm sure he's waiting to spend time with you."

Cricket smirked at her. "I'm busting a gut at your bad joke. Ha ha."

Darby made a big smooching sound with her lips. "Get outta here before I bust you in the kisser." She gave her a wink.

Cricket couldn't see where Fletcher and his boss had disappeared to, so she slipped out of the main hall to make a stop in the ladies' room.

Locals kept stopping her to praise her fare, but at last, she got to the bathroom and entered a stall, peed quickly, then went to wash her hands. Only to encounter a certain leopard who probably didn't change her spots. Too late, Cricket realized she had a security pass around her neck with her name on it, as Justine glanced down at it.

"Ahhhh... So you are the elusive fiancée Cricket?" Justine said, reaching to read her pass. She sized her up from the top of her head to the tips of her boots—dressing fancy for Cricket was a short dress with cowboy boots. At least it beat dressing like a cougar.

Cricket extended her arm to shake hands. "Hi! Cricket Ferguson. And you are?" She knew damn well who she was, but she was going to play coy.

Instead of shaking her hand, though, Justine took it upon herself to assess Cricket even more intimately. She crossed her arms and slowly strolled around her, her head following her as she turned. That uncomfortable sense of being appraised for auction made her skin prickle. Once

Justine had made a full circle around her, she paused, facing Cricket, then reached out an extended finger to the edge of her cleavage, tracing her long gel nail along the edge. It was about the weirdest thing anyone had ever done to Cricket.

"What spectacular breasts you have," Justine said, rendering Cricket speechless. "Your little Fletcher failed to tell me what a smokin' hot body his fiancée sported."

What the fuck was she supposed to say to that? She stood frozen in place, hoping like hell someone would come rescue her.

"Maybe the three of us could play together sometime," Justine said, practically purring as she leaned in closer to Cricket's ear, her fingers massaging Cricket's scalp. "Fletcher's so amazing in bed, I can only imagine how much fun it would be to add you to the tableau."

Um, what? So Fletcher had slept with her? Ewwww. Seriously? Had he no shame? And she wanted to do a threesome? With her? And Fletch? Cricket needed some disinfectant, stat.

"I'm sorry, but you've got it all wrong." Cricket primped her messed-up hair then turned and hightailed it out of the bathroom, grateful she at least peed before that unnerving encounter. She needed to escape the cray-cray lady pronto. On her way out, she ran headlong into Fletcher, who was exiting the men's room.

"Ho-ly shit," she said, grabbing Fletcher and pulling him back into the men's room then locking the door. "What the fuck is the deal with that psycho you work for?"

"I'm guessing that means you met her?"

"I didn't just meet her—I was appraised like some sexual slave and then she cooed about how much she wanted to have sex with you and me." Cricket was panting hard, anxiety overtaking her initial shock and rage. "And she said how good you were in bed. You actually *slept* with her?" She glared hard at him.

Fletcher winced as he scrubbed his hands over his face, then ran his fingers through his hair. He lifted his right hand in the air. "Cricket, I swear to God, I've never slept with her. Seriously—did you get a look at her? She's three times my age and tries to be hip and young, but she's horrible."

"Understatement of the year," Cricket moaned. "Here I was all excited to have this great contract, yet now I learn this deal has tentacles a mile long. She only did this to get her claws into me too. Likely one more way to get to you."

Fletcher pulled her into his arms. "I swear to you I won't let her near you."

"God, it was so awful, Fletch. She did this thing." She reached for his hand and pulled it toward her, guiding his pointer finger along the cleavage edge of the bodice of her dress. "She dragged her finger along here, slipping it beneath the fabric like she owned me or something. It was like nothing I've ever experienced."

"That's the last she'll do that to you, Crick. I promise. I'll go deal with her immediately."

Cricket looked down to realize that she'd literally guided Fletcher's finger on a walking tour of her breast. All of a sudden it seemed like a perfect plan.

"Umm…" Cricket said, licking her lips. "Maybe not quite yet."

Chapter Nine

FLETCHER was torn between outrage and horniness. Not two minutes ago Cricket had told him how his boss basically assaulted her, which made him want to up and punch the woman in the face. She had some nerve. But then Cricket was reenacting the offending behavior and somehow it seemed so right for his fingertip to be taking a leisurely stroll along the edge her dress, right along her tits. He couldn't believe his luck.

He looked at Cricket, who two minutes ago had outrage and fear written across her face but right now had that look of desperation that he knew from years of being with her: If she didn't get her hands on him ASAP and vice versa, she was going to explode.

Fletcher didn't, however, want to be presumptuous.

"Permission to come aboard?" he whispered into her ear.

"Provisional permission granted." She reached behind him and slid her fingers below the waistband of his jeans.

"What are the provisional conditions?" Please, God, let it be in his favor.

"That you do that thing you used to do."

He leaned in and pressed his lips to her. "Why, what thing was that?"

"This." She guided his hand beneath the edge of her dress to cup her breast, then led his other hand beneath the bottom edge of her dress, leaving him to find precisely where she needed him.

He let out a groan. "Oh God, Cricket," he said into her mouth as his fingers slid beneath the edge of her panties into her already slick center. "You're so wet."

"Just thinking about what you would do to me made me that way. I've been on edge all day fantasizing about this."

"You have been?" he said between kisses, before moving his mouth toward her breast, which he'd slipped over the edge of the bodice so his mouth would have easy access.

"It's been so long since I've had a man's hands on me, and I thought how perfect it would be to get you to fill in the void. I mean you're here, I'm here, and I sure could use the help."

His lips trailed kisses along her breast till he reached her tight nipple and his mouth latched on to suck hard. She groaned out loud, which hit him right in the cock. He could not believe he was doing this, here, now, with Cricket Ferguson. Not that they hadn't found all sorts of unusual and of-the-moment places to get off in the past—when you're young and in love and lust, you make do wherever you can. And for them, that meant all sorts of crazy places like rest stop bathrooms, the back of either of their trucks, on remote hiking trails in the park, at the drive-in movie, up against the wall in the loft of Cricket's barn. They were good at being inventive when the need arose. But he didn't want to take advantage of her, either. This needed to be mutually consensual or he'd stop, even if it killed him.

His mouth played with her nipple, and he took small bites, licking it and sucking on it till she cried out. Meanwhile the fingers of his other hand strummed along her swollen lips, circling her clit as she thrust toward his hands, encouraging him on. Her fingers fumbled with the button on his jeans then finally popped it and quickly zipped down the fly, greedily encircling his swollen cock. One touch and he thought he'd shoot his load right there, he was so turned on. "Go easy, babe," he said. "I want to make this last."

He sped up the pace of his fingers, slicking then pumping into her wet channel, mimicking what he really wanted to do with her right now, only with his cock. Cricket moaned, soft and quiet, and Fletch knew what to do, pulling hard with his mouth on her nipple as he rapidly slicked over her clit with his pointer finger. When she groaned loudly, announcing she was coming, he pumped two fingers inside of her as her channel tightened and spasmed around his fingers and she pressed her hips toward him. Christ, he needed release himself after that.

Which seemed to be a prayer that Cricket was willing to answer. No sooner did she come down from that climax than she was tugging his pants down his hips and spreading her legs. She hopped up, latching her ankles behind him and pulled her underwear aside as she eased the tip of his cock to her opening, now soaking wet with her juices, and slid herself onto him.

It was Fletch's turn to gasp. God, It had been a long time since he'd been with anyone, but he'd never been with anyone quite like Cricket since they split up. It washed back warm memories of their time together, particularly of how well they fit together, as if his cock was made to be inside of her and her alone. Once his cock was seated all the way inside her, he held her to him and pressed his forehead to hers. He flexed his cock inside her wetness, hoping she could feel what she did to him.

Slowly he began to withdraw, then quickly slammed himself into her again. He fixed his blue eyes on her green ones and silently spoke to her. "Come with me, I want to feel your pussy squeeze hard against my cock and milk every last drop of come from me."

Cricket dug her heels into his backside like she was riding a bronco and thrust her pelvis against his, grinding against him over and over until she trembled against his body. Her pussy convulsed on him as he tensed and froze, shooting his come deep within her while she came around him. Holy shit, was he glad he made the trip home.

Chapter Ten

CRICKET was unclear of the protocol for nearly being molested by your ex-boyfriend-slash-fake-fiancé's creeper woman boss and then running into the arms of said ex-boyfriend, only to slip back into old habits which were, it turns out, great habits, at least from a sexual satisfaction perspective. Because *dayum*, that man had a way with his mouth and fingers, and she hadn't felt this tingly and satiated in all the right places in ages. The only problem was they were in a men's room with a party going on outside those doors. Any minute now, his boss was likely to come in and try to join in the fun. Plus Cricket had to get back to overseeing the food situation even though she knew Darby had it all under control.

Fletcher glanced at his watch and unhooked Cricket's ankles so he could slide her down from him. She grabbed a wad of toilet paper and tucked it into her underwear to keep proof of their little tête-à-tête from leaking down her legs.

"That"—he dragged his tongue along her lips as he hiked up his pants and zippered up his jeans—"was fucking amazing." He helped her tuck her breast back inside her dress. "The only thing is now we both smell like we just had sex."

"Oh my God, you're right. What are we going to do?"

He grinned. "Enjoy it while it lasts?"

She hit his arm playfully.

"Knowing that woman, she's going to notice instantly. It's like she's some predatory animal."

His eyes widened. "Did I not try to tell you this?"

"Yes, but it seemed a bit hyperbolic."

"And now? You still think I was exaggerating?"

"Uh, she propositioned me in the bathroom. A big fat no to that." She grinned. "But the funny side effect was after she propositioned me in the ladies' room, I ran into you and pulled you into the men's room where we mutually propositioned each other."

"Maybe we can pick up where we left off later? I know Justine is going to be speaking shortly and she'll have my head if I'm not there for that. But I sure wouldn't turn down a command performance. Maybe in a more appealing venue?"

"I'll have a lot of work to do tonight, what with cleanup and stuff. Maybe a rain check?"

He grabbed her ass and squeezed. "Promise?"

She knew she was completely crazy to do this, but it was too damned good to pass up. To steal a stale cliché, how could something so wrong feel so right?

Cricket stood toward the back of the room when Justine came up to the stage. She couldn't watch her without thinking of how brazen she was and how much she seemed like a predator stalking her prey. Now Cricket knew what those poor gazelles felt like on the African savanna.

"I'd like to thank everyone in Bristol for the warm welcome," she said, lifting her hands and clapping for her audience. "And this wouldn't have happened without the suggestion of my assistant, Fletcher Campbell, local boy made good. I say assistant, but he's much more like my cabana boy, aren't you, sweet pea?" She reached out and dragged her nail along his jawline as if he was her pet. He recoiled from her touch. "So hot and so good in bed." She then reached down and spanked him once, hard, on his ass. Fletch turned ten shades of red and looked like he was about to erupt like a volcano.

What a bitch. She clearly had a mean streak and wasn't afraid to tap into it. And she was jealous that she had what she viewed as competition with Cricket, which was laughable. For one thing, Cricket and Fletch were a thing of the past, but for another, Fletch would never hook up with Justine. Aside from it being inappropriate from a boss-employee standpoint, it was beyond age-inappropriate.

Justine made some more obnoxious comments before wrapping up her talk. Cricket was grateful the woman hadn't barfed up to the audience what great tits she had. She would've died if she had.

Once the crowd began to dissipate, Cricket heard some folks in the audience cackling at the cabana boy reference.

"Wow," said one local rancher she'd known since she was a kid, a man her mother loathed because he was known for doing precisely what Justine had done to her. "Just goes to show you that you leave the country and you leave your values behind."

Cricket glared at him. She knew for a fact that man had conducted extramarital affairs for years. Who the hell was he to judge Fletch's morals?

Some older gal leaned over to her gaggle of friends. "Did you see how she smacked his ass? It was like a reverse *Fifty Shades of Gray* thing. Instead of him having all the fun, she got to. There's a couple of men I'd like to give a hard whack like that to."

Cricket wanted to tell them it was obviously no fun for Fletcher being humiliated in front of his hometown like that.

"What the hell is wrong with him, letting that woman treat him like that?" Cricket recognized that voice as belonging to Fletcher's dad, Wyatt, a rancher who never did brook much bullshit from people. Cricket liked that about him, but she was sure this would not help matters with poor Fletch. She looked around the room to try to find him, but he was gone. Rats. She figured he wanted some alone time, but more than likely, he needed some solace. She'd get things cleaned up here and track him down afterward.

Chapter Eleven

WHAT a fucking bitch Justine was, humiliating him as she had. Bad enough he wasn't getting much legit film experience working under her putative tutelage. After all, she spent far more time trying to bed him than she did explaining the ins and outs of the film industry. After that outburst, he decided he'd had enough. He slipped out a back door and started wandering the streets of his hometown, trying to make sense of his emotions: anger, rage, embarrassment, lack of fulfillment. More like D: all of the above. And sure as hell wondering what it was about living in LA that made sense at this point.

Eventually he circled back toward the theater, passing by the pâtisserie. He decided to try the door—this was Bristol, after all, where no one ever locked a damned thing up. Sure enough, the door opened for him and he stepped foot inside. Only to be met with the familiar snarl of Dingo, who faced him with bared teeth and the unmistakable sound of don't-fuck-with-me, dog style.

"It's okay," he said, trying to use a soothing voice even though he was scared to death she was going to lunge at him. What was with this dog not trusting him? He thought about that for a second and rolled his eyes. The thing was probably genetically programmed to hate him. But then again, his owner seemed to be able to get past her years of resentment, which was surprising. Lust was a powerful emotion. *Three cheers for lust.* But enough about lust—he had to focus on not being mauled by this dog in the next sixty seconds. Maybe then he could concentrate on his professional failings and whether what he was feeling for Cricket went well past sexual desire and more into emotional territory.

He'd never even given that a half a consideration; he figured he'd chosen a path and there was no turning back. But something strange happened—and fast. Whatever they did—was it only hours earlier?—was like a wildfire in intensity and impulsivity. One second they were civil and empathizing about their plight; the next minute they were like two randy teenagers who'd just discovered the joys of sex. And boy was it joyful. He closed his eyes as he reflected on the feel of his fingers slicking through her center and he moaned. Which reminded him that there was a dog at bay who might want to sink her teeth into his thigh.

"Shhhh." He kept his voice soft, trying to calm the thing. "I'm not the enemy," he continued. "If you want someone to bite, can I offer up my piece-of-shit boss perhaps? What she's lacking in meat on her bones you'll gain in the joy of injuring someone who has bad intentions for your mom."

He rolled his eyes. Talking to the dog like this? Had he lost his marbles?

"I mean, sure, I know you were led to believe I'm the bad guy. And I guess I am. Or was. But I wasn't intentionally that guy. I was trying to keep Cricket from being left suspended in amber while I created this whole new life for myself. I didn't mean to hurt her. I was young and had what I now know were foolish ambitions—that I had what it took to make it in Hollywood. Sure, I had fun when we made the film here, but what I didn't know is it had pretty much nothing to do with the business. Now, I get that there are disgusting quid pro quos all over the place there, people who expect you to put out to get ahead. It's not at all what I bargained for. I wanted to try my hand at something different and fun."

Dingo growled one of those throaty growls that can be the prelude to springing into action. Shit. He was afraid to move for fear she'd take that as a sign of his aggression. What could he do to stop her? That's when he remembered he'd stuffed a macaron he'd been eating in his pocket when Justine went off on her tangent and insulted him at the reception. He'd stormed off with no place to set it down. He reached slowly into his pocket and pulled out the now-crushed macaron and carefully crumbled a bit into his hand. First he tossed a few Scooby Snacks onto the floor between him and the dog. And thankfully Dingo responded like any self-respecting dog would, scarfing up the bits then wagging her tail for more.

"What a good girl you are," Fletcher said in a quiet voice. "You want some more cookie?" He carefully reached his hand out, fingers tucked in, to give her a chance to sniff him. Her nose nudged at his closed fingers and he gingerly opened them, allowing her to get the hidden treats inside. Quickly, he crumbled the rest of the macaron and hand-fed it to his new best friend as she wagged her tail and licked the remnants of the cookie.

"All I know is it's a damn good thing I'm not a burglar." He stroked her head. "Because you just failed simple Dog 101 there, my friend. And I didn't even have to invest in a good piece of raw steak to succeed. Lucky for me."

"Lucky indeed, or you'd have been shredded into a thousand pieces all over the floor of my lovely little pastry shop."

Fletcher turned to see Cricket standing behind him, her

arms crossed as she tapped her toe at her failed guard dog. "Who's my best girl?" She said in a high, squeaky, dog-mom voice as she bent over and Dingo came running toward her, promptly flipping onto her back for belly rubs. Cricket leaned over as the dog licked her face.

Fletcher turned and walked toward them both, watching the joy on their faces as they reunited after being apart for the evening. Man's best friend indeed.

Finally Cricket stood and faced Fletcher. "I'm sorry about what she did to you tonight."

For a minute Fletch stood there lost in thought, one hand scrubbing along his chest, the other tucked behind the nape of his neck. At last he opened his mouth to speak.

"I suppose you could say I had it coming to me." He shook his head. "I kept thinking I could work around her bullshit, but there's no working around her. This woman is playing a dirty game of chess and she's not above doing anything to win. Her profession is evidently a blood sport of sorts, and we're all pawns in a game we didn't even realize we're playing. If I had been smart, I'd have quit the job the first day she started trying to get at me. But I was too afraid I'd have to slink back home with nothing to show for my efforts. Only thing I'd have succeeded at was breaking us up and gumming up any potential career as an actor." He frowned.

"You know you can always come up with a new plan."

"Yeah but who wants to start over like I'd have to?"

"Maybe you wouldn't start over altogether. Maybe you need to reconsider your entrée into the entertainment industry."

"You mean instead of porn star, which it seems is what Justine would choose for me?"

Cricket laughed. "Well, you do have some impressive

60

moves that might skyrocket you to fame and fortune there."

"You're saying that to make me feel good."

She shook her head. "You did all that to make *me* feel good. Turnabout's fair play."

Fletcher reached out to pull her into a hug. "You know the pleasure was all mine."

She shook her head. "I beg to differ—I got a large chunk of that pleasure, thanks to you. Maybe we can call it a draw since we both seemed to come out ahead."

"Deal," he said. "Though I wouldn't object to a lightning round in case we need to prove a winner."

She laughed. "Oh, honey, I think that was already a lightning round, judging by the flashes of light I saw behind my eyes when you did that thing—"

He held up his hands. "I know you said you've got a lot of work to do, so we'd better change the subject or I might be inclined to take you right here on one of these rickety café tables."

"With all of these big windows here, that might be contraindicated unless we want to put on a show for Bristol."

"I think what you've done here is show enough for everyone in town." He pointed at the display cases of pastries in front of them. "You know I never got a close-up of your beautiful handiwork when I was here yesterday," he said, eyeing the incredible selection. "I'm no expert, but they look like fucking amazing pastries."

Cricket smiled. "If you'd like to hear what you're looking at, say the word. I love to talk about my pastries— they're like my children in a way. Only less disobedient."

He thrust out his lower lip. "Remember how we used to talk about one day when we had children together?"

She frowned. "Yeah. Although nothing personal, but I've tried since then to block that from my memories."

He reached for her hand and held it, palm up. Pressing his fingertip to the surface of her palm, he slowly traced a spiraling trail.

"What're you doing?"

Her breathing accelerated; she must have liked it. He wasn't sure what he was doing, but it felt right. And he remembered that this was an erogenous zone for Cricket, so there was that.

"I wanted to have some contact with your skin. Something you'd view as harmless but nonetheless tactile."

"O-kay…"

"So talk to me about your children here." He pointed to the cases filled with shiny, colorful, tasty treats.

She smiled. "While it's not Rebecca and James and Samantha—"

"Sammy."

"Yeah, well, that was yet to be determined, the last I heard." He nodded. "These aren't my flesh and blood, per se, but they are a labor of love nonetheless." She pointed to the case nearest the door. "Over there, I've got the usual suspects: tart au citron, pain au chocolate, Paris-Brest, gateau, and éclairs." She pointed to the center case. "There you'll find mille-feuille, and macarons. There are nougat macaron and kiwi and orange canelle, but the raspberry's my favorite. Then there's a plaisir sucré—which means sugar pleasure."

"I hear the French know all about pleasure."

She rolled her eyes. "If my memory serves, you weren't completely ignorant to that yourself. But I digress." She pointed to the next row of pastries. "Over there you'll find the petit kouign-amann, the financiers, the tarte tatin, tarte aux fraises or framboises or citron, the Saint-Honoré, and the canelé. And to drink, we offer such French classics as café au lait or chocolat chaud.

"I never thought I'd live to see such decadence in our little town," he said. "But I like it. By the way, I find it incredibly sexy when you speak French."

"*Mais oui*," she said, grinning.

"Talk dirty to me in French," he said, pulling her closer to him, their hands clasped.

"*Voulez-vous coucher avec moi, ce soir?*"

"That's from a song," he said.

She nodded. "It also seems to be an anthem to my new carefree attitude. I mean, look at me—I went from loathing you to fucking you in a matter of hours, right? I was so worried it was a bad idea, but now I see that I can enjoy just having sex with you without tangling it up with old emotions. I realize it falls under the category of 'fun while it lasts,' but the truth is, I haven't had any fun like this in such a long time, I'm totally up for indulging if it feels as good as it felt back there." She pointed down the street toward the theater.

And while Fletcher wasn't convinced they no longer harbored more intense feelings for one another, for the time being he'd take what he could get from Cricket, ferocious dog and all.

Chapter Twelve

"SO does that mean you would be willing to do it on the shop floor?" He grinned. "A man can hope, right?"

"I'm not ready to put on a show for all of Bristol. But the good news is"—she pointed to a door that led to the staircase to her apartment—"privacy is a mere flight of stairs away."

"Would it be asking too much if I grab a pastry or two to replenish my energy stores?"

"Be my guest. *Après vous.*" She motioned to the case and grabbed a few plates to place them on.

He moaned. "I told you your speaking French is an incredible turn-on."

"Well then, choose something and hurry up so I can put my linguistic skills to work."

He arched a brow. "If that involves your tongue, I'm on it."

As he reached for something, he held up a cup for her to identify: inside was something creamy with chocolate.

"Mousse au chocolat," she said as he licked his lips. "Grab two of them."

Next he held up a layered pastry of cake, nuts, candy, and chocolate with chocolate whipped cream topping. "I believe you called this sugar pleasure, two of my favorite things."

She nodded. "Ahhh... Plaisir sucré. A good choice—

dacquoise cake with hazelnuts, praline, and milk chocolate."

Finally he held up a palm-sized tart. "One of my favorites," she said. "Tarte aux citron. Filled with lemon curd, which makes me happy."

"If it makes you happy, it makes me even happier. Now come on." He reached for her hand as he balanced a plate filled with pastries in the other. "There's sugar pleasure to be had."

She led him up the flight of steps, with Dingo on his heels. Luckily the dog had abandoned her suspicions of the man and was willing to follow him anywhere for food. Such a girl after her own heart.

They got to the top step and Cricket opened the door to reveal a warm, cozy living room with cheery lemon-colored walls and an overstuffed sofa in porcelain blue. The wide-planked oak hardwood floors were finished in a warm umber. In one corner stood a fireplace with an oak mantle. A pair of French doors opened to a small balcony with an Italian tile-topped wrought iron table.

"Wow," Fletch said. "All yours? So grown up. I'm still living in a shitty furnished studio apartment which comes with complimentary cockroaches."

"The worst kind of roommates."

"Tell me about it."

She went to the sofa and sat down, patting the seat next to her. Fletch placed the sweets on the coffee table in front of them. "It's funny, but you and I never were roommates despite being together so long."

"My loss."

She nodded. "Not gonna argue with you."

"Have you had interesting roomies?"

She rolled her eyes. "In Paris, I roomed with a man who went clubbing each night till four in the morning."

His eyes widened. "You roomed with a man? A complete stranger?"

"It wasn't cheap living in Paris. I had to find a way to make it work. I found a guy online and he seemed fine enough."

"Was he in the program with you?"

She shook her head. "Actually, he was a model and kept crazy hours and barely ate a thing. On weekends when I'd be in the apartment practicing my cooking, I tried so hard to encourage him to sample my goods, but he couldn't eat because of his job."

"I thought that was a female model thing."

"Nope, guys too."

"So did you and he…" He twisted his pointer and middle fingers together in an apparent international sign of having sex.

"Is that what men think? That if a woman is living with a man, she has to be his concubine or something?"

"Concubine? Yeah, like right out of *Lawrence of Arabia*."

"It seems to me that if I were a guy living with an attractive woman, it wouldn't take long for me to want to do her."

"Spoken like a true guy."

"Maybe because I am a true guy."

"It didn't cross my mind to have sex with him, but it was a moot point since he was gay."

Fletch heaved a sigh of relief. It didn't escape Cricket's observations how oddly possessive he was for a man who'd chosen to end their relationship of his own accord.

"While you're mulling the myriad possibilities of me having roommate sex with strange men, why don't you try some of these pastries. Maybe it'll get your mind off of it."

Though to be honest she enjoyed that it must have

bothered him. Serves him right.

He took a bite of the plaisir sucré and let out a moan. "Holy shit, is that good," he said between mouthfuls. "Sugar and pleasure all wrapped up in one. I know only one thing that could make it better." He raised an eyebrow at her, but instead, she handed him the lemon tart.

"Try this and tell me what you think."

Fletcher sank his teeth into the buttery pastry. There was something about lemon curd that satisfied the deepest hunger pangs in her. It was always her test of someone to see if they, too, felt as passionately about it.

He stopped midbite and looked at her, then crooked his finger to coax her to him. When their faces were inches apart, he leaned over to kiss her, his mouth still nursing the lemon tart. That cunning man. It didn't bother her for a second that he decided to share the tarte au citron in a most unconventional way.

Their tongues twined over the tangy, sweet, salty combination and it gave Cricket pause to realize he couldn't have responded in a better way to her offering.

Eventually their lips parted as they came up for air.

"You know most people would have offered up a forkful of that rather than sharing it off their tongue."

He grinned. "Since when have I been most people, Crick?"

"Yeah, good point. I can't wait to see how imaginative you might get with the mousse au chocolat." She winked at him.

"Expect the unexpected." He reached for her hand and clasped it in his, covering his other hand over it as well.

They sat for a few minutes in silence, the sound of Dingo snoring the only thing to break the quietude.

"So was it worth it?"

He looked at her, puzzlement in his eyes.

"What we did back there?" He pointed in the direction of the theater.

She blurted out a laugh. "Of course not. That was totally worth it. Especially since this is no-strings, all-fun, no-worries week. I meant you're up and going to LA: severing ties, moving away, ending *us*."

He frowned. "That's not an easy question to answer. I mean, did I need to try it out?" He shrugged. "I suppose I did. Otherwise I'd never have done something as dramatic as ending us." He pulled her closer. "Do I regret that now?" He looked down at her and kissed her forehead gently. "More than you can imagine. But life is all about choices and decisions and sometimes they end up being shitty ones and you're stuck living with the consequences for the rest of your life."

She nodded slowly. "Or sometimes you take action based on the shitty decisions of others and carve out a new life for yourself that is if not better, then at least more inventive than the one you'd imagined."

He cocked an eyebrow. "If this were a competition, I'd have to admit you won, hands down."

"We're not in a race, Fletch," she said, twirling her finger in the hair on his arm. "Maybe you're a late bloomer with this career thing."

He pouted. "Or maybe I gave it a try and it wasn't what I'd expected it to be."

"Did you have many chances to act in LA?"

He shook his head. "I gave it a shot. Let's say I waited a lot of tables." They both laughed. "But I did take a couple of screenwriting classes and if anything, that's been the most interesting aspect of this business to me."

"You're writing things now?" She considered that for a

moment. "That makes sense now that I think about it. You always were a gifted writer."

"Thanks. I guess I had enough freelance gigs under my belt to make me feel like a legitimate writer before I pulled an about-face and tried to plunge into acting."

"You make it sound like you were impulsive in your decision to do that."

Dingo hopped up to join them on the sofa and he reached over to scratch her head. "And dog makes three?"

"You'd be surprised how much a dog can warm you up on a cold, lonely night."

"Fair enough."

"So have you had a lot of other women?"

"I'm not sure 'had' is the correct verb. It sounds a little conqueror-like, as if I colonized women along the way."

"You're avoiding the question."

He shook his head. "No, I'm not. To be honest, I've dated on and off a little here and there, but there's been no one special in my life." He paused, looking at her. "Would it sound trite if I said no one matched your high standards?"

"Trying to earn brownie points?"

"Would it be foolish if I were?"

"Foolish? No. Unnecessary? Absolutely. Water under the bridge at this point. Now it's all about superficial sex, minus emotions and all of that messy stuff. So technically it's irrelevant. I'm no more entitled to be upset about who you've been with and what you've done than you are about me."

"So you've had other lovers?"

She laughed. "Such a very French way of phrasing that. You sure you weren't the one who lived in Paris?"

"You're avoiding the question."

"Touché. Okay, so were there other 'lovers'?" She made

air quotes to tease him.

"I'm not sure I want to know."

"There was a time when I went out with guys and even slept with them for my own little emotional revenge. I know that sounds childish of me. But I guess I adopted an 'I'll show him' attitude."

"And did you?"

"Did I what?"

"Show me?"

"I don't know. Is it too late to know if it bothered you that I had sex with several other men to avenge your breaking up with me the way you did?"

He heaved a sigh. "It bothers me immensely."

She knit her brows. "That's so caveman of you."

"I don't know if it's caveman, or if it's a foolish guy who fucked up and now regrets it massively. A guy who realizes too late what he gave up and maybe wants to prove he can learn from his mistakes." He leaned forward and began planting kisses along her collarbone. "It makes me want to make up for lost time." His tongue followed the trail begun by his lips as he moved down her body. Lifting her dress over her head, he circled her taut belly with his mouth as he worked his way toward his very own pot of gold. He shimmied her panties down past her hips, then slid his hands beneath her bottom, spreading her legs wide with his shoulders. He glanced up at her, licking his lips. "Mine," he said as he lowered his mouth, his tongue spread wide to capture as much of her essence as possible on the first pass.

Cricket jumped as his tongue pressed to her spread lips, and she let out a sigh of contentment. Soon she began to grind her hips toward his mouth, encouraging him to linger each time he found a sweet spot. She wove her fingers through his hair, massaging his scalp while gently directing his mouth with her silent commands.

"My God, you've got a talented tongue."

"The better to lick you with, my dear," he said, lifting his head and grinning at her. Cricket let out a moan, knowing deep down in her heart that the more intimate things became with the two of them, the harder it was going to be for her to make the break when it was time for Fletch to return to his life. But did that stop her? Hell no.

Not for the first time would she wonder if she'd made the right decision to pretend that her feelings weren't going to come into play. Something told her she'd made a big damned mistake.

Chapter Thirteen

FLETCHER wasn't quite sure when it had finally dawned on him that he and Cricket had a whole lot of unfinished business to attend to. Not only that, but also that he had no intention of finishing whatever business they needed to deal with. Each minute he was spending with her reminded him that he'd been a flaming asshole to walk away from what they had. Was he worthy of her at this point? Did he deserve to win her back? He didn't have the answers but he sure as hell planned to try his damnedest.

In the meantime, he'd woo her with what he'd like to believe were his own inimitable skills, coupled with a little creativity and imagination. He reached for one of the cups of chocolate mousse on the nearby coffee table. Lifting his mouth from Cricket's center, he scooped two fingers into the dessert and painted it right down where his tongue had been. Cricket squealed and giggled as he smeared the cold concoction along her lips, then settled his tongue back along her clit to lap at the dessert.

"Oh, you naughty boy," she said on a moan as he circled his tongue around her clit. She pressed herself toward him, encouraging him onward as his fingers slid inside her while he sucked.

"You're quite an amazing chef," he said as he lifted his head to fix his eyes on hers, which were hazed over with lust.

"And you're a most imaginative lover." She pulled his

head against her center, her hips circling faster until her climax broke, her vaginal walls spasming against his fingers as she released a flood of juices to mix with the sweet chocolate.

Only after she came did it dawn on Fletcher that if he wasn't careful, she'd have chocolate mousse all over her nice sofa. So he lifted her up and carried her to the kitchen, where he sat her on the island as he quickly shed his pants and notched his hard cock to her opening, chocolate and all. He lifted her legs till her feet hit the countertop and spread her legs wide to allow him in. This gave him a bird's-eye view of his cock sliding into her slick opening, her pussy swallowing him inside, and his cock hardened at the sight. Jesus, he wanted to take this woman every way that he could to show her how much he wanted her, how much he realized he needed her. He only hoped it wasn't too late.

Fletch leaned over and grabbed a nipple into his mouth as he pumped himself into Cricket. He began to play with her clit with one hand, despite her protestations.

"I can't, Fletch. Too soon. Too sensitive."

"You can do it, Cricket. Feel how hard I am inside you? That's how much I want you, how much I want to feel your pussy convulsing around my cock, pulling the come from me."

Just thinking about it made him crazy with desire and he clutched her hips hard, driving himself deep inside her until the tension mounted to the breaking point, pins and needles giving way to a wash of relief as he released himself into her for the second time in only a handful of hours.

He could get used to this.

Cricket had an old-fashioned claw-footed tub in her bathroom, which looked out onto the mountains, illuminated by the bright, full moon. That's where Fletch realized right here, right now, for the first time in forever he felt at home. And home was naked in a bubble bath with Cricket's beautiful ass nestled up against his cock as warm water sloshed against them and she leaned back into his arms, carefree and sexy as hell.

"Can I ask you something?" he said as he twirled a finger through her hair.

"Fire away."

"How did you manage to get it all so very right?"

She turned to look at him.

"What do you mean?"

"I mean all this. A successful business, a beautiful home, a serenity about you that says you know what you're doing and you're doing it, no questions asked."

She thought for a minute. "Gosh. I never really thought about it," she said. "I mean after you left, I was a hot mess for a good while. I spent a lot of time crying. Ask my mother. She probably could have wrung water out of her shirt for as many times as I cried on her shoulder. But then one day I had clarity. I knew I needed to get away from the scene of our lives together. I knew I loved to cook things, so why not say 'fuck it' and get myself to Paris? I didn't know a soul, could barely speak the language, but there is quite a bit of revelation when you put yourself so far beyond your comfort zone. You start to know what to do and when to do it." She reached for the wineglass she'd placed on a table next to the tub and took a sip. "Before I knew it, I was carving a life for myself and making it happen."

"Was pastry school hard?"

She laughed. "Hell yeah, it was hard. My idea of baking

and their idea of baking were two entirely different things. But I rose to the challenge and graduated at the top of my class. I earned the most challenging internship and stayed on for six months there to complete it. I'd have stayed longer if I could have gotten a job; it's not easy to get work permits for the long term."

He shook his head. "I admire the hell out of you for having pursued this and worked it out, no muss, no fuss. Then coming back here and opening your own business, and, well, look at it."

"Thanks, Fletch. That means a lot to me."

"I'm sincere about this. You amaze me."

"You'll probably lose your level of awe once we learn that Justine has decided to crush me like a bug since I wouldn't submit to a threesome with her."

"The mere mention of her name has a magical ability to shrivel my dick to Lilliputian proportions."

She giggled.

"But seriously, my future progeny owe a debt of gratitude to you, being that they were in peril due to permanent shrinkage that occurred in the presence of my boss."

"Meanwhile, you haven't seen her since you left her hours ago after her intentional public shaming of you, have you?"

He nodded. "Yeah, and I'm not sure if I'm even going to go back to work for her. I'm over her bullshit, you know?"

"Can't say that I blame you. With bosses like her, who needs prison cells? Working under her is like a life sentence of psychological incarceration. I appreciate that you set goals for yourself and all, but suffering through that crazy bitch on a daily basis is hardly worth it."

He nodded. "I'm starting to realize there comes a point

when self-preservation needs to stop taking a back seat to career ambitions."

"Well, if you need some help while you're figuring things out, I'm happy to let you bounce ideas off me."

He reached his arms around her and turned her around so she sat facing him.

"But for now, the only bouncing I want to experience is when I get to watch your luscious tits bouncing as you ride my hard cock. Deal?"

"I'd like nothing better." She leaned over and placed her lips over his, her tongue finding its way into his mouth, exploring and stroking along his tongue as she ground her center along the length of his cock. It swelled in no time. Soon he guided it inside her and clutched her hips and went along for the ride as she bucked, lifted, and plunged down again on his dick. He closed his eyes, savoring the moment, realizing that he had some choices to make: the same mistake he made last time, abandoning this for the hollow world he would return to in LA, or figure out a way to convince Cricket that they still had that unmistakable magic, that they could rekindle the flame and make it burn brighter than ever before. That with age and maturity came the recognition that what they had was a once-in-a-lifetime thing and wasn't something to toss away like he'd done so foolishly before.

Chapter Fourteen

FOR lack of a better plan of action, Fletcher chose to simply ghost Justine rather than deal with her bullshit. He knew it was making her absolutely insane. By the time he'd turned off his phone, he'd piled up at least thirteen calls and forty-two text messages from her, each one increasingly hysterical and nasty.

"You will never eat lunch in this town again if you don't reply to me immediately," she'd said in the last one. Which made him laugh. If by "this town" she meant Bristol, he figured the likelihood was greater that she'd never eat lunch here again if he had his way. Over the past two days, he'd gone from humiliated to empowered as he ran into old friends and even some relatives he'd not seen in a while, all of whom were indignant at how she'd treated him at the reception.

Rumors, of course, had run amok that Fletcher was some sort of gigolo, lending himself out for astronomical prices to further his career ambitions in Hollywood. When he heard someone voice that at Annie Bananie's Pie Emporium, he was tempted to grab a chocolate cream pie and smash it into the guy's face. It was one of those country boys who came into town to eat, he presumed when they got tired of parboiling varmints they trapped in their raccoon traps.

"Hey, Cabana Boy," the one guy shouted at him. He

thought it was Luther Morrison, some loser he'd gone to high school with, but if it was, the guy hadn't aged well, what with the long, straggly hair, beer gut, and nicotine-stained teeth. "Maybe you can teach me the tricks of the trade so I can become a famous Hollywood gigolo too!"

It took Fletcher all the restraint he could muster, but he maintained his dignity and refrained from the pie assault, as fun as that would have been. He knew revenge was a dish best served cold to that meth head, and he'd been working feverishly over the past few days on his very own form of revenge. He hadn't even told Cricket what his plans were.

Speaking of Cricket, she'd invited him to join her parents for dinner back at the ranch tonight. At first he was reluctant to agree—no doubt her folks had certain opinions about him that weren't about to change anytime soon. But he knew if he had any chance of fixing things with Cricket, they were going to have to be on board. Same with Darby. Team Cricket wasn't going to allow him to ever cause her soul to ache again, and he needed to prove it to them.

Before picking Cricket up, he stopped to get a bottle of wine for her mother and her dad's favorite bourbon, plus a bouquet of flowers. Then he diverted to Annie Bananie's to pick up a banana cream pie, which he knew her parents loved. He was covering all his bases.

He picked Cricket up a few minutes before six, and once again was on the receiving end of Darby's stink-eye. She did that thing where she pointed at him, pointed at her eyes with two fingers, then pointed back at him, so he would know she was watching his every move. Shy of writing on a chalkboard one thousand times "I will never hurt your best friend Cricket again," he wasn't sure how to make it okay with her. Only time would tell.

As they drove out to the ranch, Cricket told him about

her encounter with Justine earlier in the day.

He clenched his jaw as she filled him in.

"So she stopped by right after lunch," she said. "She had on a leather minidress, because, well, who doesn't wear a short leather dress in Bristol?" She grinned. "Oh and thigh-high boots, which are always the right thing to wear in a cow town too."

Fletch rolled his eyes. The woman was insufferable.

"She came in when Darby was still at lunch, but Dingo was lying near the door. Of course the minute that thing stepped inside the shop, Dingo started barking like crazy. Justine had a look of abject terror in her eyes. I have to admit I enjoyed watching her crap a brick or two over it, especially because I know Dingo wouldn't hurt a flea. Her bark is way worse than her bite since she doesn't even have a bite."

"Now you tell me."

Cricket laughed. "She's my greatest ally."

He nodded. "Yeah, between her and Darby, you can be assured no one will bother you ever."

"Darby can be a bit overprotective."

"Gee, ya think?"

Cricket knitted her brows. "Why do you say that like that?"

"Maybe because she threatened to shish kebab my nuts if I hurt you."

Cricket burst out laughing and clapped her hands together. "Oh, goodness! That's why I love that girl so."

"Yeah, I'll leave it at I respect her for loving you."

"Let's get back to Jerky Justine... So I called off Dingo, and immediately she seemed to have gotten her groove back. She strode in like she owned the place, demanded to see you, and told me she knew we weren't engaged, but she still thought we could all have a lovely time together at a skinny-dipping party at her swimming pool with some guy named Paco."

"Paco? The guy who delivers the drinks at the pool?"

She shrugged. "Sounds like he does more than serve drinks. Good to know she's an equal opportunity sexual harasser at least."

"And what did you tell her?"

"Well, that's when she started getting creepy."

He lifted an eyebrow. "Started? I hate to tell you we're well past that now."

"Good point. The other night it was creepy enough when she was stroking along my breast. But today she put her face right up to mine and angled her head and started to freaking kiss me!"

Fletcher thought his head might explode. "What the fuck?"

"I know, right? But then the best thing happened."

"Please tell me your dog bit her."

"Even better."

"I'm on pins and needles—what?"

"Darby walked in as this happened and I squealed out loud and started banging on Justine's shoulders and was trying to push her away and Darby came up from behind and pulled her off of me and hauled back and punched her!"

"Right in the face?"

Justine nodded rapidly. "Bloodied up her nose!"

"I knew I liked that friend of yours."

"She's a prince, that one is. But don't ever get on her bad side."

He rolled his eyes. "Trust me, I'm well aware of that."

Chapter Fifteen

"I'M having flashbacks being back at your folks' place," Fletch said. He pointed to the barn. "How many times did we sneak off to the loft when we wanted to be alone."

She cocked a brow. "Is that what they call it now—'being alone'?" She elbowed him in the ribs.

"I'd pay good money to slip away there right now to get you alone for a few minutes."

"You and me both. But Mom's got a rib roast waiting and she said you'd best bring an appetite."

Fletch licked his lips. "She made a rib roast? But I thought your mother hated me."

She scruffed her fingers through his hair. "I thought I hated you too, and look at me now."

He smiled. "I guess there's hope for us all."

They walked hand in hand up the walkway to the house and Cricket called out to her parents in the foyer.

"Mom, Dad—look what the cat dragged in."

Her mom, Linda, was a tall, blond, blue-eyed woman with the healthy, tanned look of someone whose body agrees with outdoor living. Her father, Bob, had a full head of silver hair and dressed like the lifelong rancher he was, in blue jeans and flannel and boots.

"Fletcher—so good to see you." Her mom reached out and pulled him into a hug.

"Mrs. Ferguson, the pleasure is all mine."

"Fletch." Her dad extended his hand and gave him a nod of acknowledgment, which might as well have been like passing him a peace pipe. No way would he have shaken hands with Fletch if he was pissed at him.

"Mr. Ferguson," Fletch said. "Thank you for allowing me to spend time with your daughter." Which sounded a little weird, considering she was all grown up and not even living at home, so it was not as if permission were required, but Cricket figured he was trying to be conciliatory, and with her father, it would work. He only wanted his daughter to be happy, and both of her parents could see that she'd had an extra spring in her step since this loose reunion with Fletch occurred.

Over cocktails on the back porch, which overlooked the mountains of Glacier National Park, they discussed such compelling matters as the price of hay and which horse was going to be bred with which horse next go-round. It was all so normal, Cricket could hardly believe they were here as if nothing had ever changed. Yet it had. A lot of pain and heartache, but she'd come through the crucible and landed in a much better place. If Fletch hadn't let her go, maybe she'd have stagnated here in Bristol, never expanding her horizons, never seeing a bit of the world, never learning a skill that would make her so happy. Oddly enough, perhaps Fletcher's leaving her was a gift.

It was dark when they finished up dinner and finally left Cricket's folks' place. As they drove down the long driveway, Fletch reached for her hand and laced his fingers through hers. He lifted their hands up and glanced at the cheap ring she still wore on her left ring finger.

"You know, it sort of looks like it belongs there," he said, spinning it on her finger with his thumb as he drove.

Cricket cocked her head toward him. "You think so?"

He nodded. "Except that it makes me realize all the more what a fool I was to give up on us like I did."

"You'll get no argument from me." She grinned at him.

"Way to be supportive."

"Just calling it as I see it." She squeezed his hand. "But seriously—I said before that I got over it and truly, I have gotten over it. And I grew as a result. So while it sucked—I mean it really, really sucked, you jerk!—I took away important lessons, so let's not minimize that. Besides, what's done is done."

"And maybe I can do other things to make amends for that?"

"Such as?"

"Such as… let me sleep on it. But in the meantime, I was thinking." He turned off the car's headlights as they approached the barn so as not to arouse suspicion with her parents in case they looked out to see them turning in instead of heading out to the road. "Maybe now's the time to rechristen the hayloft. It seems the right thing to do under the circumstances."

She arched her brow. "And what circumstances would that be?"

"Well, the circumstances in which we've both rediscovered one another and realized that even though everything's changed, deep down inside, nothing important has."

"So, in honor of that, we do it in the barn?"

"You have a better idea?"

She shook her head. "It might be a little chilly in there. They're calling for frost tonight, you know."

"I think we know how to stay warm."

Fletch gave Bunny a pat on the flank as they walked by the horses on their way to the stairs leading up to the loft.

"It'll be like old times," he said as they climbed the stairs. "Heavy breathing from us and the sounds of horses down below." He pulled Cricket toward him and draped his arms around her neck.

"What makes you think there will be heavy breathing going on up here?"

"How about I prove it?" He settled his mouth over hers and she opened her lips to receive him, his tongue tracing a path through her mouth before tangling with her tongue.

"How about you stop talking and start doing?" She laughed into his mouth.

"I aim to please." He picked her up and walked her to the wall then began to kiss her again. Light from the full moon streamed in through a nearby window. The soft chuff of the horses below was a welcome accompaniment to the intensifying sound of their breathing. Fletch quickly shoved up Cricket's skirt, unbuttoned his jeans, and shoved them to his ankles as Cricket hoisted herself up and around his waist. "This is going to be quick, though, to be sure we get in and out before being caught."

"I need it to be quick because I want to feel you inside me, now," she said, her tongue licking a trail along his chin toward his ear.

"Shit, Cricket, you know that drives me crazy."

She nibbled along the shell of his ear and let her tongue follow along.

"I aim to please," she said with a grin as he slid himself into her wet center on a gasp.

Cricket was breathless with the sensation of him filling her.

"This," he said, beginning the slow withdrawal, then slamming back into her, pinning her against the wall. "Finally I'm home."

With that he quickened the pace, one hand beneath her ass, the other sliding farther up her dress to find her peaked nipples. He squeezed a nipple hard between his thumb and forefinger and she squealed in pleasure. Then Cricket slid a hand down to where they were joined, slicking her finger along her clit.

"Fuck, Crick, that is so incredibly sexy."

She was out of words, so caught up in the pleasure and sensations, the slide of his cock inside her filling her completely, the edge of a climax taunting her.

"I'm close, Fletch."

He buried himself balls deep in her and pumped in and out, then back in once, twice, eventually coming as she released, her body jerking in pleasure alongside his.

It might have been a weird time to realize it, but it was then that Cricket knew she wanted more than a quick fling with this man she'd loved so deeply for so long. She had no idea if that was even a possibility. And he sure as hell wasn't showing his hand.

Chapter Sixteen

FLETCH was reluctant to let anyone know what he'd been working on in secret. It seemed such a long shot to imagine he'd write a screenplay good enough to actually sell. But in truth, he was writing this because he had to write it, to record and process everything that had happened to him since he'd started working for Justine. This was the kind of titillating storyline that could possibly sell. And if he helped others trapped in a workplace hell like this, he'd be thrilled to have done his part. Now that he'd figured out the ending, he wanted some affirmation that it wasn't complete shit. So he was going to ask Cricket to take a look at it.

But he had one thing he had to take care of first.

After dropping Cricket back at her place, he told her he had some work to do and left, heading to the outskirts of town in search of his old classmate Luther Morrison.

Luther wasn't hard to find—Fletch figured he'd be at his local bar tying one on, and sure enough he was propping up the bar, a shot and a beer and several empties in front of him.

"The stupid sonofabitch," he was saying to the

bartender, who must have heard it all before from Luther and was busy cleaning up and wiping down the bar instead of paying much attention to him.

Fletcher sat down next to Luther and ordered a beer. He leaned over to Luther.

"Howdy, Luth," he said, nodding his way. "I hear you had something to say about me and my boss."

The smell of liquor was overpowering, and it was clear this guy lived for his next drink. Which would be perfect for his plan. Luther wouldn't give a shit about the repercussions of his actions. As long as his reward was looming.

"I was just saying I'd make a better gigolo than you would." His eyes were practically rolling back in his head, and he wobbled a bit on the barstool.

"I agree completely," Fletch said. "Which is why I'm sending you on a mission to prove yourself to her."

Luther sat back and gave him a once-over. "Me?"

Fletch gave him a broad smile. "I think Justine's sick and tired of me. She'd love to try some local blood. And who better than you?"

"That's what I've been saying. Isn't that right, Jimmy?"

The bartender looked at him and nodded, then went back to work.

"Here's all you have to do." Fletcher wrote down the address of the inn where Justine was staying on a piece of paper and handed it to Luther. "Now Justine loves a good pie. She was expecting me to deliver some to her room, but I know she'll be thrilled if you do it instead of me. So tomorrow morning when Annie's opens for breakfast, you need to be there promptly at six a.m. so you can get the Boston crème pie before they run out. You're gonna take that pie down to the inn, and I'll let the caretaker know to expect you and that you've got permission to deliver it directly to her room. Justine will be waiting for you and she'll be putty in your hands if you bring her that pie."

He stared at Luther. "You think you can follow those easy instructions?"

Luther returned a glassy-eyed stare. "What's in it for me?"

Fletch grinned. "As if an hour of pure bliss with Justine weren't enough, I'll throw in a fifth of Jack Daniels for you once you let me know your mission has been accomplished."

Luther nodded slowly.

"You need me to write down your instructions?"

Luther leaned his head back incredulously. "You think I'm some sort of dumbass or something?"

"Oh, hell no," Fletch said, grinning. "I only pick the best for Justine. And I know she's gonna love what you have to offer her."

"How do I get my Jack?"

"I'll be waiting outside in my truck, a block away. You look for me and report back, and the Jack is yours. Deal?"

Luther nodded. "I love a good bottle of Jack."

Anything indeed.

Fletch left the bar and headed over to his parents' place. He'd been staying in town because of his work commitments but suddenly needed to sit and talk with his mom, even if it was after ten o'clock. The good thing is he frequently got emails that his mother sent at three in the morning so she'd become quite the night owl. His dad was up with the roosters and Fletch figured he'd already be fast asleep.

He parked his car and entered through the back door

into the kitchen, where his mother was in the middle of baking pumpkin bread. Like who cooks pumpkin bread at that hour of the night? Not that it mattered—he hoped they had vanilla ice cream in the freezer so he could eat some straight out of the oven with a fat scoop of ice cream to melt over top of it. And he hoped it wasn't that low-fat, low-sugar crap that tasted like garbage—nothing about dessert should ever be low anything, in his opinion. Which made him think about Cricket's pastries. Boy, he sure could use some more of that chocolate mousse, in precisely the same way he'd used it before. The possibilities of what they could do together with her dessert prowess and his imagination were downright endless.

"Fletcher!" His mom came running over to greet him. "I'm so glad you finally found some time to get out here."

"I'm sorry I didn't have a chance to get over here earlier. Things have been a bit crazy."

His mom turned on the electric tea kettle to make him some tea, and they sat down at the table in the breakfast room.

His mother leaned in a bit and lifted an eyebrow. "So… what's going on with you and work? Is this still a thing for you? Or did you tell that woman where to go?"

He scrubbed his hands over his face. "Let's just say it's been an enlightening week," he said, quirking a brow. "And with clarity comes action."

"Sounds cryptic." She got up to pour water into a mug for him and added a tea bag.

"Or possibly empowering."

"Does that mean you're not going to fill me in on anything?"

He shrugged. "I'm thinking of moving back home."

Her eyes grew wide. "Oh, really?"

89

He nodded. "I think I've had my fill of trying to make it in Hollywood, Mom." As he talked, he drummed his fingers on the table. "It's a bit of a cesspool out there. At least for me, it has been. It's not fulfilling. Sure I didn't achieve my goals, but sometimes you have to recognize that things don't always work out the way you intended them to."

She tipped her head toward him. "Are you okay with that?"

"More than okay."

"I can't say I'd be sad to see you quit that job. That woman is horrible and I was close to smacking her upside the head myself at the reception. I tried to find you afterward, but you'd disappeared. I've since speculated a bit as to where you might have gone. Which leads me to my next question: might this have something to do with someone else as well?"

He heaved a sigh. "I didn't know if you had noticed."

"Not like you've been around us this week. But it's a small town and word spreads fast."

Fletch blushed. "You think this is really messed up, don't you?"

She leaned over and scratched his head. "Oh, sweetie. Heavens no. Not even remotely." She sighed. "Fact is, while I understood what you did by breaking up with her originally, I have to admit it broke my heart a bit. I'd be thrilled if you two got back together."

He shrugged. "I've been thinking long and hard about this. And aside from hating myself for what I did to Cricket, I want nothing more than to get back to where we were. Or find a new place to be that is as good if not better. But... the problem is Cricket is viewing this as a short-term thing and then we go our separate ways." He sipped his tea.

His mother laughed. "So you're her booty call?"

Fletcher choked on the tea and spat it out on the kitchen table. "Mom!"

"Oh please, Fletcher. I've been around the block a few times. I'm not oblivious to reality. And I know that Cricket hasn't had a man in her life for a long time. Sometimes a girl has needs."

"Mom!"

"So what's the problem?"

"I think we have different agendas. First off, I realized too late that I still feel strongly for her. And I'm miserable with my life choices right now. But I don't even know what I'm going to do with myself—it's like I'm flapping in the wind. And I don't know that it's fair to impose myself on Cricket now that things are so messed up for me."

"You're being too hard on yourself." She placed her hand on top of his. "Just because you're unsure about your career doesn't mean you're some sort of untouchable. If anything, you've learned a lot about yourself through this exercise, and you've done some serious soul-searching. To me, this makes you even more special."

"Then would you mind telling Cricket that?"

She laughed. "Have you had a talk with her about things?"

He frowned. "Only when we first discussed what this thing was about."

"Sounds like over the course of the week it's changed quite a bit."

"Seems hasty, though, doesn't it?"

"I might say yes if you hadn't spent so many years together before. To me it sounds like you've both matured and you're realizing what you want. That's a good thing, baby doll."

He finished his last sip of tea and pushed away from the

table. "I've got to get going. But I appreciate your advice, Mom. It means a lot to me."

She stood up and gave him a tight hug. "I'm always here for you, Fletch." She winked at him. "And I'm rooting for you and Cricket getting back together."

Chapter Seventeen

FLETCHER pulled his laptop out of his backpack and went to the pastry shop. It was late, but he hoped he could catch Cricket before she went to bed. He knocked quietly and of course Dingo came charging down the steps and started barking like crazy. Cricket followed in her cute pajama shorts and cami top. She looked a little bleary-eyed.

"I'm so sorry I woke you," he said. "But I've got something I want to share with you."

She rubbed her eyes. "No worries. What is it?"

He pulled out his laptop. "This."

She stared at it. "A… laptop…"

"No—it's what's inside. Something I've been working on."

"What is it?"

"A screenplay."

"Really?"

He nodded. "I've been working on it a bit on the side."

"What's it about?"

He grinned. "It's about a creepy producer who sexually harasses everyone in her orbit."

"Oh, so it's autobiographical?"

"Maybe. Ish. Only in this one, there's a great revenge scene."

"Cool." She squinted. "I mean not cool that she sexually harasses you but that you've found a way to channel that.

And maybe you can make some money off of it."

He lifted an eyebrow. "That's my dream."

She gave him a quick peck on the lips. "I think you can. I can't wait to read it."

"Good—I'll expect a report on it by morning."

She laughed. "Yeah, right."

He squinted at her. "I wasn't kidding."

She arched her eyebrow. "Okay... I was enjoying my sleep, but..."

He started to laugh. "Gotcha."

She rolled her eyes. "Jerk!"

He leaned toward her and kissed her forehead. "Go back to sleep. I've got something I've got to do. We'll talk in the morning."

As Fletcher walked away, he couldn't help but think how it would have felt right at that moment to have told her he loved her. As if he'd had a dope slap over the head, it finally dawned on him that not only did he love Cricket Ferguson, but he'd never stopped loving her. The question was, could she ever love him again?

Fletch returned to his folks' house for a few hours of shut-eye before the early start he had planned for the morning. His dad was already on his second cup of coffee as Fletch attempted to slip out of the house before dawn. His father poured a cup and handed it to his son.

Fletcher held up his hands. "Thanks, Dad, but I have somewhere I've got to be."

His father wrinkled his forehead. "At five thirty in the morning?"

Fletch shook his head. "I know, implausible, but believe me, I have no choice in the matter."

His dad stirred two big spoonfuls of sugar into his coffee and enough milk to turn it white, then took a sip.

"Does this have something to do with that woman?"

He held his thumb and forefinger about an inch apart. "Can you maybe narrow that down a bit?"

His dad grunted. "That woman you work for."

Fletch's eyes opened wide. "How'd you know?"

"I didn't but can't imagine why else you'd be sneaking out before dawn except if you're up to no good."

Fletcher chuckled. "Not to worry, Dad. It's more like I want to bear witness to something." He took a sip of his coffee.

His dad held up his hands. "Son, don't get me wrong. I'm fine if you're planning on teaching that woman a lesson. She needs her comeuppance, no doubt about it." His dad gave him two thumbs up. "I knew you had it in you."

"Yeah, no worry, Dad. I wasn't gonna let her treat me like shit forever and get away with it."

Fletch looked at the clock and got up. His father patted his shoulder with a meaty hand. "Good luck, son."

Fletcher turned around and hugged his dad. "Thanks. I think it'll work out fine."

At six on the nose, Fletcher pulled up across the street from the inn and turned the car off to wait. Not ten minutes later he saw that idiot Luther weaving his way down the street, then stumbling up the front porch of the inn. He'd called over the night before, after he knew Justine would be asleep, to make sure Luther had authorization to enter the room this morning.

He watched him enter the building, then a few minutes later saw the light go on in the room over the front of the inn where he knew Justine was staying. For amusement's sake, he started counting backward from a hundred.

"Fifty-nine, fifty-eight, fifty-seven," he said, watching the front door as he drummed his fingers on the dashboard. He pulled out his phone and opened to the camera, pointing it toward the inn. Then he heard a loud crash and Luther racing down the steps, a nearly naked Justine, pie smeared across her bruised nose, hot on his tail. Fletch slunk down in his seat to avoid having his boss see him, all the while enjoying the fireworks. It was priceless to see her in such a state, and he could only imagine how badly Justine flipped out when Luther disrupted her beauty sleep with that pie. He knew she would go apeshit on him—with good reason—and he figured the minute she started freaking out on Luther he'd take that pie and lob it at her. Clearly things went according to plan. He wasn't going to lose too much sleep having set Luther up for this scenario. He was perfectly happy mocking Fletcher about Justine; now he got to see what a charmer she was in person. So much for his career as a gigolo.

Fletcher pulled a U-turn to slip out as soon as Justine stopped chasing Luther at the end of the block; then he looped around a block away and tracked Luther down, whistling to him out the window and passing him the bottle of Jack he'd promised.

Luther unscrewed the cap and took a fat swig. "Man that woman is a real bitch."

"Tell me something I don't know," Fletch said as he put the gear into drive. "Thanks for your help, Luth."

Luther nodded. "Thanks for the Jack."

"Any time. Any time at all."

Chapter Eighteen

CRICKET was finishing up reading Fletch's screenplay when he showed up at the pastry shop. Darby was working downstairs and let him in.

She pointed to the ceiling. "She's upstairs."

He nodded and took the stairs two at a time till he was greeted at the entrance to her apartment by Dingo, who jumped up, her paws on his chest, tail wagging.

Cricket leaned against the wall, arms crossed. "Well, well, well, what a difference a few days make." She nodded toward her dog. "From guard dog to welcome wagon."'

"Good to know the best pastries in town will work on even the most obstinate dog."

Cricket grinned, then elbowed him in the ribs. "Hey," she said, reaching for his laptop. "So I stayed up all night reading this thing."

"What'd you think about it?"

"I think it's fucking awesome." She wrapped her arms around his neck and planted a kiss on his lips.

"Seriously?"

Her eyes twinkled. "Do you think I'd lie to you?"

"Well, if there was any doubt, I was prepared to bribe you with pastries."

"No need. This is a terrific story. Funny and poignant and superbly written."

"You think it has legs?"

"Hell yeah," she said. "Though I don't think I'd pitch it to Justine."

He laughed as Darby came to the door.

"Knock, knock," she said, pretending to knock but walking right in.

"Morning," Cricket said. "What's up?"

"Thought you'd like to know I fielded a call from a certain psycho queen named Justine." She grinned.

"Really?" Cricket said. "Calling about the event tomorrow night?"

"You might say."

"But?"

"But she's canceled on us."

Cricket lifted her brow. "What?"

"She was a little hysterical. Or enraged. Hard to say. She was in an Uber on her way to the airport."

"Airport?" Fletcher said.

"Something happened to her. She's pissed. She said she hates this town and she couldn't wait to get the hell out."

"So there's not gonna be a premiere?" Cricket said. "What about my breakout job?"

Fletch looked at her. "Seriously, even if you have to eat the cost of this thing, consider yourself spared."

"I wonder what happened, why she chose to skip town?" Cricket said.

Fletcher started chuckling, then filled them in on what he'd set up. They all had a good laugh at the idea of a nearly naked Justine being smacked in the face with a crème pie.

"Karma's a bitch."

"And so is Justine," Darby said, roughing up Dingo's fur and getting her all rowdy till she started barking in agreement.

Fletcher thrust out his lower lip in a pout.

"Why the long face?" Cricket said, stroking his hair. "You bummed you have to go back to work now?"

He shook his head. "Actually, no. I tendered my resignation this morning. By text message."

Cricket clapped her hands. "That's fantastic! But what does that mean for you? You should be happy, right?"

He reached for her left hand and pulled it toward him, holding it up to inspect her cheap fake engagement ring. "I'm sad this means you'll be taking off our engagement ring now."

Cricket pursed her lips. "I guess no need keep it on anymore, eh?" Her face fell.

"Oh, stop it you two," Darby said. "This is my cue to get the hell out of here before things get icky." She turned and took the steps back down to the café.

"I have to admit it seems bittersweet that you'll be taking it off now, Crick."

She nodded. "Same here."

"But I was thinking..." He paused. "Maybe the next time I slip a ring on your finger, it'll be the real thing. And maybe then you'll have forgiven me enough to say yes?"

Crickets eyes filled with tears. "Are you serious?"

He leaned over and pulled her into a hug. "I've never been more serious about anything in my life. I have no idea what I'm going to do professionally, but for the first time in my life I know who I can't live without *in* my life, and that's you." He slid the ring off her finger, then kissed where it had been. "Next time—and it won't be long, I can promise you that—it's going to be for real and forever. Because I love you, Cricket Ferguson, and I can't wait to take my time falling even more deeply in love with you."

Thank you so much for reading *Cabana Boy!* I hope you enjoyed it! If so, please help others find this book:

1. Help other people find this book by writing a review.

2. Sign up for my new releases email so you can find out about the next book as soon as it's available and get fun giveaways.
   http://eepurl.com/baaewn

3. Like my Facebook page.
   www.facebook.com/jennygardinerbooks

And I love to hear from readers! Let me know what you think about my books! You can write to me at jenny@jennygardiner.net, and visit me on the web at www.jennygardiner.net.

Keep reading for a sample from Bird Dog – the next book in the **Confessions of a Chick Magnet** series.

Bird Dog

By

Jenny Gardiner

Chapter One

ELISE Jackson groaned as she stood smack dab in the middle of Main Street and reluctantly let Candy Patterson tie a blindfold around her eyes.

"Really?" she muttered as her thick blond hair got tangled into the knot with a tight tug. "Blindfolded?" She let out a growl. "This bridal party forced frivolity thing is starting to pluck my last nerve."

Candy patted her on the back, which wasn't the least bit reassuring.

"Now, now. Trust me, it'll be fine. All we need to do is follow these directions and all will be right with the world. It says: *Do something intimate with a strange man, then have your picture taken with him and post it on Instagram.* We'll do this, knock out the final thing on the list, and then we can get busy drinking martinis."

At the rate things were going, Elise was gonna need to be two-fisted with those cocktails.

"Can you define 'intimate'? I mean am I supposed to get down on my knees and give some dude a blow job for the cause?"

Candy laughed. "Have faith, Elise. How long have we known each other? Do you really think I'd make you do something like that?"

She wanted to give her a deadpan look but she was blindfolded. "Let's just say 'no comment.'"

Candy burst out laughing. "Thanks for that ringing vote of confidence." She placed her hands behind her former college roommate and steered her over to the street corner, where a group of people had suddenly started to gather. "Hugs for Henry," she said aloud as she read a sign tacked onto the lamppost.

"What's that?" Elise said.

"I dunno. There's this sign hanging up with a picture of some cute kid who must be Henry and people have lined up to hug a couple of handsome men. Not sure why. But that seems kinda intimate, no?"

"And doesn't even involved a strange guy's dick in my mouth. It's a win-win if you ask me. Quick get me in line to hug one of these idiots and let's get outta here. I'm starting to feel claustrophobic with this thing pressing up on my eyeballs. And it's so far over my nose I can't comfortably breathe."

They were on the final step of a bachelorette party scavenger hunt that had found the two of them blowing up condom balloons with a couple of guys coming out of Nick's Delicatessen; persuading a strange dad of two small children to sing "Like a Virgin" along with them as they pretended to be back-up singers; and asking a sixty-something woman to write sex advice on a cocktail napkin for Jennifer Lipton, the bride-to-be-slash-college friend Elise was thinking of disavowing at this point.

These supposedly wacky adventures were part of Jennifer's bachelorette party fun and games extravaganza, all of which only served to reinforce in Elise's mind that she was one hundred percent down with a quickie elopement *sans* all of those nuptial-related frills that she had grown completely sick to death of after having attended and/or partaken in at least ten weddings in the past year alone. That is if she ever got married, which was about as high up on her priority list as having emergency dental surgery, so a bit of a moot point.

Candy kept ushering Elise forward in line until finally they got up to what must've been the front of it, because now some guy was speaking to them.

"Aha, we've got a little Fifty Shades action here?" the guy said. Ugh, the last thing Elise wanted was for someone to think she was some sort of S&M fan-girl.

"Yeah, I'm so desperate for a bit of bondage I even walk down the street blindfolded," she said, snarling her lip. "I was just bummed my friend here left my ball gag back in the hotel room."

"I see you've got yourself a sassy one," the guy said, giving her a nod.

"Yeah, sorry. She's a little cranky right now," Candy said. "See, we're on a bachelorette party scavenger hunt. My friend here has to do something intimate with a strange man and then Instagram the picture. Because I'm a trusty friend, I'm going to keep it PG-rated and nothing that would humiliate the poor thing. Besides, she's got a bit of anxiety about this thing around her head, so please, be gentle."

Elise could hear the guy rubbing his hands together. She kind of felt like a stallion with blinders on about to be auctioned to the highest bidder.

"Cool. Cool," he said. "Just so you know, I don't normally hang out on street corners hugging people, but my friend's kid Henry needs some surgery and they just lost their insurance and can't afford it. So a bunch of us decided we'd do a fundraiser hugging people to raise money to help Henry out."

"Oh, my God, that is so sweet," Candy said. "Isn't it sweet, Elise?"

Elise had kind of lost her warm fuzzies over this project. "It is sweet, and I hope Henry gets his day in the O.R. Now can we get on with this so I can remove this blindfold before a full-blown panic attack sets in?"

"Your friend's a little testy, eh?"

"Seriously she's not normally like this. I think she's officially wedding'd out and the blindfold was the proverbial straw that broke the camel's back. After this we get to go drink, so we're totally incentivized to get it over with and move on to the real fun."

"In that case, let's do it."

"Oh, but Elise, you really should see this cute dog that just waddled over to us."

"That's my buddy, Sherlock," the guy said, leaning over to scruff the dog's head.

"What kind of dog is he?"

"He's a Basset Hound."

"I could eat him up with a spoon, with those hang-dog droopy eyes and the ears—Elise, they go all the way to the ground!"

"Well, crap. You know now I have to pet the dog." She pursed her lips, trying to figure out the logistics. "Here—help me so I don't fall flat on my face." She reached out her hand to steady herself on her friend as she bent down. Candy guided her hand to the dog's head. "That's a good puppy." She puckered up her lips and let the dog lick her face as she made kissy noises to him while he slurped his tongue along her face. Finally, she stood up, dusting her hands off on her jeans. "Okay, now let's get this done with so I can actually see the dog and give him the proper attention he deserves." She paused, her hands on her hips. "How exactly does this work?"

"Well normally when two people hug, one reaches out

opened arms and wraps them around the other person, whose arms are also extended. They clasp, hold tight, then release."

"Oh, we've got ourselves a real rocket scientist here today," she said, opening her arms. "Alrighty, then. Arms open wide," she spread her arms wide. "So let's insert Tab A into Slot B already."

Just then she felt a warm body press up against hers in a manner she hadn't felt in far too long. And then warm arms that snaked around her body, pulling her tightly up toward his. Against her better judgment she could feel herself sinking into hard chest—how could she not, he felt so very yin to her yang? But yikes—was that... his Tab A she was noticing, suddenly nudging its way practically against her Slot B? Because whoa, that was so not okay. Even though it felt kind of like old home day for some bizarre reason. But no, she could not be pressed up against a stranger who was rapidly growing a hard-on. In broad daylight. Without her even seeing the guy. Ewww. Even if he did have a supposedly cute dog.

Elise stiffened at the, well, stiffness, diplomatically pulling back from the man before he embarrassed himself on her, or worse, she embarrassed herself right back by being more receptive than the occasion dictated.

"Okay, then," she said, shoving her hands in her pockets, making it clear the touching thing was over. "I'm all good to take this thing off, Candy? Let's get that picture and vamoose."

Candy worked to loosen the tight knot behind her until finally Elise was able to draw it over her head. She squinted and rubbed her eyes as they were suddenly accosted by brightness, then opened them to see standing before her the man who owned the most prime piece of real estate on her

Shit List: Wilson T. Montgomery. The high school boyfriend who took her virginity then dumped her in the douchiest of ways, leaving her reeling and weeping and hating the very soil he walked on for years afterwards.

"You!" she said, her eyes wide, pointing at him as if fingering a criminal. "How dare you touch me with your grubby little paws."

"Elise?" he said, his brows furrowed as he stared at her. "That was *you* beneath that blindfold the whole time?"

"Oh, my God, I can't believe you touched me with your, your, your *cooties!*" Not beneath making a scene, Elise shrieked.

He lifted a brow. "Cooties? What the hell are you talking about?"

"You know damned well what I'm talking about." She grabbed for Candy's hand. "Let's get out of here. Now!"

"Wait a second," he said. "You can't leave yet."

"Why not?"

"Because you have to pay up." He pointed to a woman who sat nearby with a cash box. "That'll be fifty bucks."

"Fifty bucks? To hug the guy who ditched me on prom night for slutty Samantha Cadbury, who never met a guy she didn't do on the first half of a date? For that matter, even if wasn't her damned date to begin with?"

He shrugged. "First of all, you are talking nonsense. Second of all, you agreed to the hug, and we hugged. You did the crime, you gotta do the time."

She glared at him as she pulled money out of her wallet and slapped it on the little card table where the cashier worked.

"I'm only doing this so that little Henry gets his surgery. By the way—for what it's worth, hugging you was like hugging a cactus: stiff and prickly."

"Oh yeah? Well maybe you needed something stiff in your life."

"I'll show you stiff," she said, rearing back as her arm seemed to get a mind of its own, powering her hand across his face, with a loud smacking sound. "Something I should've done years ago, buster."

With that, she stormed across the central plaza, not even bothering to wait to take the requisite photo for Instagram.

Chapter Two

WILL was starting to get into the rhythm of this hugging-for-dollars thing. At first when his friend Ricardo had suggested it, he laughed it off.

"As if people would pay us to hug them."

"Seriously, we put a poster up with a picture of Henry with those puppy dog eyes, I'm telling you women will be on us like white on rice."

Will cocked an eyebrow. "So, are you in this for the philanthropy, or to cop a feel or two with rando women?"

His friend grinned. "Can't we do both?"

They high-fived each other as they figured out the simple logistics to get the project underway. They were all together in town for the next few days for their friend Jamie Gusskind's wedding. Will hadn't been back home to Bristol, Montana for years—his family had all moved away, so there wasn't much of a draw to returning. Except of course the breathtaking beauty of the craggy mountains and acres of wildflower meadows dotting the valley below. He'd forgotten how much he'd loved this place, and was grateful he'd have a few days to soak it all in before he had to head back to the real world.

What he hadn't expected was his old science teacher from middle school throwing down fifty bucks to hug him, or one of his mother's old bridge partners, who asked on his folks, who'd followed the sun to Florida once his father retired from the National Park Service. Having a dad who was a ranger had been pretty awesome growing up, and as kids he and his brother and sister got to enjoy the outdoor life in a way most kids didn't, even in a town in which pretty much everyone spent the bulk of their free time—and often even work—outside, reveling in nature.

After the fourth woman old enough to be his mother extracted a hug from him, he leaned over to Roberto.

"Dude," he said. "Here we thought this was gonna be cop-a-feel day on Main Street. Or at least have a couple women who were easy on the eyes," he scraped his fingers through his wavy, black hair. "What do we have to do to get women our age to come over here?"

His buddy nodded toward two women crossing the street.

"If you build it, they will come." He winked. "There's the answer to your prayers, my friend."

Will eyed the blonde, who was maybe three inches shorter than his six-foot build. That was where any comparison stopped: where he was hard, she was soft. Where he was solid, she was curvy, with long, lithe runner's legs, a narrow waist and a set of perky tits that filled out her body-hugging shirt to a T. His gaze wandered to her face but a blindfold basically covered half of it up, so there was no telling what she looked like under that mask. No matters: he wasn't looking for a date to the prom. He just wanted to while away the next hour or so wrapping his arms around a bunch of hot women, raise some money, have some fun— what wasn't to like about that plan?

"I call dibs on the blonde," he said before his friend got a chance to stake his claim.

"Fine, but you're buying first three rounds tonight."

Which was kind of a rip-off because Roberto was technically not officially allowed to want to grope women, since he'd been dating his girlfriend Michelle for months now.

By the time the blonde finally made it to the front of the line, Will had also hugged an eight-year-old girl, someone's cat, and a grandpa.

He greeted the blindfolded woman and her guide with a broad smile.

Up close the woman was even more smokin' hot. He was going to have to restrain himself or he'd have his palms all over her gorgeous heart-shaped ass before he knew it. Meanwhile, every word she uttered out of her mouth was so snarky, he immediately wanted to angle his mouth over her smartass one. Too bad he couldn't get a good look at her face—between the blindfold and the glare from the sun it was hard to get a good bead on what she looked like, but damn, that body was rocking, with those high, pert tits that were impossible not to ogle, and the form-fitting jeans taunting him with her tight, hot little body.

Will gave a quick whistle and his dog Sherlock loped over to where they were talking, and the brunette started oohing and ahhing over him. Chicks loved that dog. Then again, who wouldn't? He was the most perfect four-legged creature he'd ever encountered. Of course he was biased.

The women loved on Sherlock for a bit but seemed in a hurry to get on with the hug. The blonde stood up and asked what next, so he told her the drill. Maybe he was being a bit of a smartass himself, but she'd already played that card so he was just following suit.

When she finally piped down and he slid his arms around her waist, he could feel the weight of the world slip away from him. Here he was, embracing a woman he didn't even know, but he had this burning desire to do exactly what she'd snarkily said to him not thirty seconds ago: insert his Tab A into her Slot B. It did not help matters that the closer his body insinuated itself up against hers, the more his, er, moving parts shifted, like a tree bending toward the warm sunlight. Shit, what a time to get a hard-on. There was no distracting himself with math calculations or mental images of his sister's wedding even. Because all he could think about were her soft tits pressed so close to his hard chest, with only a millimeter or so of fabric keeping them from being skin to skin. And if things were different—like, say, if he even knew this woman, right about now he'd be groping for the button at her waist and tugging the zipper down and before either of them could count to ten he'd have been pressed so deep inside of her, their heads would be spinning. So strange—how could he be overreacting so much to this woman he didn't even know?

He was vaguely aware of the brunette popping off a bunch of pictures on her phone, but he just couldn't even have given a care about that. As long as she wasn't Instagramming pictures of him naked, it was all good.

Inexplicably, though, the mood shifted, and the blonde peeled back suddenly, retreating from this tight, warm, embrace, instead backing away like she'd touched a hot stove. Shit, clearly his physiological reaction clearly spooked her, which was kind of sucky because it's not like he willed himself to grow hard while pressed up against her. Hard not to, haha.

Lost in thought, he barely realized what was going on until he saw the blindfold drawn away from her face.

"You!" she shrieked at him, pointing at him accusatorily. "How dare you touch me with your grubby little paws?"

"Elise?" he said, his brows furrowed as he stared at her. "That was you beneath that blindfold the whole time?"

What the what? Elise Jackson? The woman he lost his virginity to? The one who flipped her shit at him halfway through prom night when she accused him of banging Samantha Cadbury even though what he was actually doing was comforting her after her date had left to go to a party out on someone's ranch and never came back. And wait a minute—Elise, a blonde? When did that happen? Shit, she looked sexy as a blonde.

Well it was no fucking wonder he wanted to have this woman. And why his dick responded to her like some Pavlovian dog. All these years had passed and yet still, something about her called to him. Even though they'd parted ways practically enemies so many years ago—she unwilling to hear any reason, he just sick and tired of trying to get through her thick skull and finally just giving up. And now this.

And before he had a minute to process exactly how best to negotiate some sort of it's-been-ten-years-let's-start-again kind of truce, the woman wound up and slapped him across his cheek. Damn. He wasn't sure which was crazier—that he stood there, not responding to what she'd just done, his hand pressed to his smarting face, or that all he could think about was if this was the price to get her back, then maybe he was willing to pay it.

Bird Dog

Coming March 12, 2019

About the Author

Jenny Gardiner is the author of #1 Kindle Bestseller *Slim to None* and the award-winning novel *Sleeping with Ward Cleaver*. Her latest works are the *It's Reigning Men* series, the *Royal Romeos* series, the *Falling for Mr. Wrong* series and her new *Confessions of a Chick Magnet* series. She also published the memoir *Winging It: A Memoir of Caring for a Vengeful Parrot Who's Determined to Kill Me,* now re-titled *Bite Me: a Parrot, a Family and a Whole Lot of Flesh Wounds*; the novels *Anywhere but Here, Where the Heart Is*; the essay collection *Naked Man on Main Street*, and *Accidentally on Purpose* and *Compromising Positions* (writing as Erin Delany); and is a contributor to the humorous dog anthology *I'm Not the Biggest Bitch in This Relationship*.

Her work has been found in Ladies Home Journal, the Washington Post, Marie-Claire.com, and on NPR's Day to Day. She was also a columnist for Charlottesville's Daily Progress for over a decade, and is the Volunteer Coordinator for the Virginia Film Festival.

She has worked as a professional photographer, an orthodontic assistant (learning quite readily that she was not cut out for a career in polyester), a waitress (probably her highest-paying job), a TV reporter, a pre-obituary writer, as well as a publicist to a United States Senator (where she first learned to write fiction). She's photographed Prince Charles (and her assistant husband got him to chuckle!), Elizabeth Taylor, and the president of Uganda. She and her family and menagerie of pets now live a less exotic life in Virginia.

Visit Jenny at her website and sign up for her newsletter, her blog, or find her on Facebook and Twitter. And every blue moon she'll post adorable pictures of her pets on Instagram as @thejennygardiner.